A DOWRY OF SNAILS AND MUD

BRITTANY TUCKER

A Dowry of Snails and Mud

First edition: January 2023

Copyright © 2023 by Brittany Tucker DBA First Fruit Press 2022

All rights reserved.

No part of this book may be reproduced in any form or by any electronic or mechanical means, including information storage and retrieval systems, without written permission from the author, except for the use of brief quotations in a book review.

This book is a work of fiction. While historical, artistic licensing has been taken for entertainment purposes.

Cover Art by Miblart

Illustrations by Ashley Lambright

ISBN: 979-8-9864878-0-9—Ebook

ISBN: 979-8-9864878-1-6—Paperback

ISBN: 979-8-9864878-2-3—Hardback

❀ Created with Vellum

To my baby Lily.
Never be ashamed of the dazzling gazelle you are.

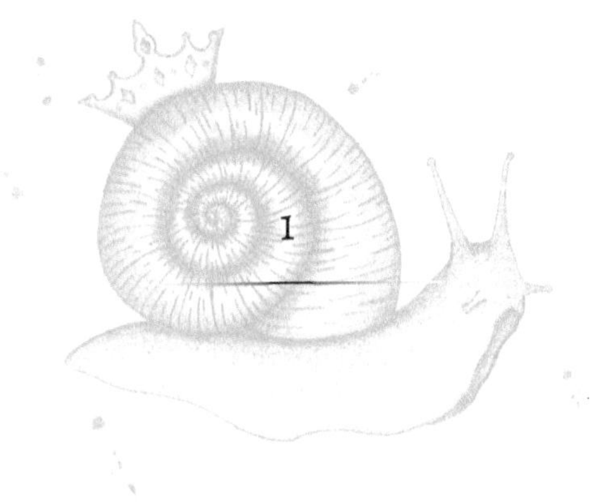

"On the subject of mollusks."

I hate snails. That's the sum of it.

They're awful, gritty, gummy, invasive pests.

I plucked a particularly obese specimen out of the mud, rolling it between my fingertips. How would it feel to crush it, to let the shell crack beneath my chipped nails? *Do they pop like ripe plums, or melt like slugs?* Questions for later.

Instead of committing a murder, I tossed the defenseless creature into my bucket with a sigh, sending it to join the doomed fate of its brothers and sisters. I glared up at the sky. It had always done a tremendous job of matching my mood, and today wasn't the exception—gray, bland, and a wee bit testy.

Ice cold raindrops fell, seemingly at random, but somehow still managed to strike the tip of my nose. At this point, the weather hadn't convinced me of its neutrality.

"You shouldn't scowl at them." My twin brother, Drystan, picked through a patch of reeds. For a moment, I wondered if he meant my aerial attackers or the snails. He sniffed. "It's not polite."

I arched a brow. Drystan grinned at me, his golden-blonde hair, and dark, blue eyes the same color as mine. I snatched a snail from my bucket and chucked it at him. "Is this polite?" A second snail went airborne. "How about this?"

Drystan caught the projectile vermin, then pouted as he cupped them in his palm, stroking their spiral shells. "Your misery isn't their fault. Leave them be."

"They're getting eaten either way. Manners won't save them."

Drystan huffed. "Roasted or not, Rhia, you should be kind to your subjects." His shoulders slumped. "But I guess—by the end of tomorrow—we'll all be your subjects, won't we?"

I stood, ignoring the creak in my lower back, nausea rolling through my insides.

Subjects. I'll have subjects, responsibilities. I'll have a husb—

I shook my head to chase the thought away. *Not now. Not today.* I turned to my brother, forcing a fake smile. "Let's get these back to Papa. I've had enough of wading around in this slop."

Drystan nodded and followed me out of the mudflats—a two-acre flat chunk of land on the outskirts of my village, infested with the round, crunchy critters. We used to farm potatoes in the flats, but with all the rain in the last few years, the ground had congealed into an algae-filled swamp—no more potatoes.

The lush, beautiful Wentwood forest surrounded the fields, calling to me as we walked, whispering that I should find out just how deep its rabbit holes could go. I ached to feel the bark of oak and ash, to smell the ferns curling out of the earth. I could escape. Just keep running until a less burdensome life found me, or I disappeared completely. I wasn't sure which sounded better.

But the forests weren't safe anymore, and we couldn't hunt.

Not when invaders loomed just beneath the shadows of the canopy, and they'd stolen all our weapons. I'd put arrows through their eyes if we had any, but arrowheads require steel, and steel required money.

We didn't have either.

As Drystan and I moved across the flats, muck splattered my trouser legs and threatened to suck the boots straight off my feet. I grimaced. *This may be my last day wearing pants.* It would be all gowns and petticoats from now on.

I glanced at the dirt packed beneath my nails, staining my fingers, matching the murky browns of the village ahead—Lians. My home, the only home I'd ever known. The Wentwood forest connected the regions of Monmouthshire and Gwent, and Lians sat just at the latter's border. I'd grown up surrounded by trees. Earth, bark, and leaves inhabited every part of my soul.

As the oldest community in the region of Gwent—a providence in southeast Wales—and far from the King and his royal city, Lians had been here for centuries. Sure, there were other villages, but they'd turned to a nomadic way of life—trekking to the lowlands in the cold months, then to the highlands in the summer. Moving flocks, gaining their income from outside trade. I'd heard some of them had even gone as far as to barter with foreigners on the coasts.

But not my people. We were hardy, had overcome every adversity thrown our way, and would continue to do so for hundreds of years more.

At least, I'd always thought so—and Papa never failed to remind us of it, again and again. *We are not kneelers.* He'd say when we were young, sprawled in his armchair, wiping ale foam from his mustache. *We don't kiss bottom, scrape boots, or spread sugar on what we say and do. You are a Caddell, Rhia, and you bow to no one.*

I thought those words would protect me, and I often

repeated them in the night, wrapped in my threadbare blanket as the wind howled through the cracks in our rattling windows.

But now, a part of the royal city was coming here—*for me*—and it felt like one big joke. Except, I wasn't laughing.

We continued our walk in silence, heavy pails clicking against our knees. I tried to ignore the worried glances Drystan sent my way every few paces, as if he expected me to vanish into a mist at any moment. I supposed that's how it must feel—like he is about to lose me.

And in a way, he was. A class-fueled barrier would always linger between us now. Creating resentment, creating distance.

All because I'd soon be marrying a Crown Prince of Wales.

———

Let's go for a tour, shall we?

If you could view it from above, Lians would look like an oversized carriage wheel. Town Hall sat at the center—an ancient, round pine-log construction surrounded by hitching posts and hay troughs. Not that we needed them. In total, there were three horses in Lians—all owned by my father, the mayor. Worn dirt streets stretched off in every direction from the Hall, leading to the different "districts"—if you could call them that.

The village's west side consisted of the blacksmith, a carpenter, a stonemason, and a butcher—all owned by the same families for generations.

The East and South sides were homes—all cut stone, bare windows, and thatch rooves. The North held our meager livestock barns and adjoining pens. What few sheep we owned were used for meat and wool. Even on the rare occasion we did have an abundance, Papa refused to trade.

Despite its age, Lians wasn't large. Some of the younger villages in Gwent had expanded to having thousands of residents, but not us. Our sloppy roads were a hazard to the few precious wagons we owned—used to haul crops to and from the fields—and moving between towns would endanger their delicate wheels. So, everyone walked instead. Each town and village elected its own mayor, who served as leader. My ancestors served as mayor since Lians' founding.

Some princes or another controlled many of Wales' regions, but not Gwent. None wanted to travel so far south, especially when the King's current residence, Aberaron, lay in the western region of Ceredigion, by the sea.

I do feel obligated to tell you that Wales doesn't really have a *king*. Just a prince, who rules in place of the King of England, then continues to spawn gaggles of potential, future princes. But, for simplicity's sake though, we'll call the head prince the King, and not all of his "princes" are sons. Some are appointed, allowed to rule smaller regions. All of them are a nuisance.

Lians may not be much, but it's mine, and I know every tree, twig, and root. Every incline and slope in the landscape. No one could take that from me—that deep-rooted sense of belonging to the land. *You are a Caddell, and you bow to no one.*

Smoke billowed from Town Hall's chimney, along with steam as raindrops hit the hot stones. Trystan opened the main doors, and a glorious wave of burning air slapped me in the face, greedily sucking the moisture off my damp skin. After a moment, my eyes adjusted to the dim lights and dryness. Despite our low supply of candles, I counted ten lit and randomly placed on the Hall's encircling floor-to-ceiling shelves —what little light they gave absorbing into the dark cherry walls.

As we moved inside, I curled up like a pill bug to find a place to stand between all the sweaty bodies. Every face in the village had arrived to help prepare for the most dreaded—I mean— exciting event in Lians' history.

My wedding.

As others noticed my arrival, I managed to grin back at the

cordial smiles that greeted me. Pleasant, but not friendly. I'm sure most of them would have loved to knock my teeth out. They weren't any happier for the coming ceremony than I was.

Catching sight of Papa, Drystan and I pressed against the wall, sidling through the crowd until we'd reached the opposite end of the room. A massive, rounded hearth towered in the center of the Hall, customarily surrounded by benches so the villagers could gather to keep warm during the cold months. Now the benches sat in lined rows to be used as tables, the hearth commissioned for cooking and boiling water instead of just a toe heater.

Papa smiled at us as we approached—in all his round-bellied glory, complimented by his thinning blonde hair and chipped peg-leg. The mayor of Lians—and the reason it had to be *me* getting married tomorrow.

Let me explain.

Papa stopped paying the King's tax years ago. *Refused* would be a better word. If the King couldn't protect us and feed us when we starved, why should he pay him? *What does that flat bottomed prick know of toiling in the soil?* He'd rant. *Has he ever felt the sun beating on his back, knowing his crack would be pink by the end of the day, and keep working despite? I think not. I can't respect a man that's never had a burnt crack.*

And Papa got away with it, for a time . . .

Until the King demanded the gold due to him, and Papa refused. The King continued to insist, and Papa continued to decline.

And the spiral went on and on, until one day, Papa got a letter—the prince, the King's sixth son, would be here by the end of the month to take my hand. Papa was furious. Mama said I should see it as an honor, but the entire village and I saw it for what it was—a trap.

If we refused the proposal and insulted the King, that would be a good enough excuse to wipe Lians off the map without drawing any sour looks from his lords. If we accepted, he got to rid himself of an extra son while also sending someone to force us into submission.

Little did the prince know, I wasn't the only one who'd refuse to bow. My people didn't take well to strangers. He was in for the ride of his life.

"About time you trouts showed up," Papa gruffed, taking our buckets. "I was starting to wonder if the mudflats finally swallowed you both whole." He winked. "I hate being wrong—and here I hoped I'd have two less mouths to feed."

"If only." I rolled my eyes. "I'd take being eaten by a mud monster over what's to come any day."

Papa's lips pursed, avoiding my gaze, as he set our new crop of snails aside for washing. Later, we'd haul them to the castle for boiling.

Yes, Lians has its very own castle. No, it doesn't have a name, so don't ask. Why name something without a purpose? It's a ruin now, but after tomorrow it would be my home. *Maybe I'll come up with a title later.* I smiled to myself. *The pit of despair? No, no, that's already taken.*

I glanced around, sucking in a deep breath. There were so many snails to be washed. It would take all night. I didn't feel like spending my last evening as a free woman shoving my fingers in nasty, stinking shell holes. *Unless . . .* I crossed my arms and batted my lashes. "Have you seen Mama?"

Papa nodded, stirring a bubbling cauldron that contained the malted grain recipe he used for ale, by the smell. "She's helping with the vegetables." He sniffed at the steaming water then made a face. "Lord above, what I'd give for real drink. You'd think *someone* in this blasted region would know how to make a good ale. If only your grandfather were still alive. God rest his brewer's soul."

"Can you get Mama for me?" My words came out sharp, but

I managed to twist them into a croon, making Drystan raise a brow. I ignored him. "My feet are killing me."

Papa blinked, startled. It wasn't often I asked for things from him outright. Everyone else? Sure. But not him, being the man of the house, and all. He wiped his muddy hands onto his pant legs. "A-all right. Hold on."

Once he'd hobbled out of eyeshot, I grinned at my brother, nodding toward the full pails. "Help me load these on the wagon, would you?"

Drystan's brows rose even higher, wrinkling his forehead. "But they're disgusting."

"I know." My grin widened. "Let my dear, sweet prince enjoy a mouthful of grit. It's good for his health, you know. Very cleansing for the bowels."

It took a moment, but Drystan's smile matched mine. "You realize we all have to eat those, right?"

I shrugged. "It won't kill you, but it will be wonderfully satisfying for me."

"You're a terror."

Another shrug. "No more than you."

"The girls cooking will see the dirt."

"And you'll tell them to ignore it." I gestured to our haul. "After you."

Drystan lifted two of the pails, shaking his head. "How your new husband will love you so."

All smiles died from my lips.

Husband. The word echoed painfully through my mind. *I'm not ready.*

Even if sixteen was a perfectly average age to marry in Wales —the exact age Mama and Papa wed—but that didn't mean it's what I wanted. What I'd dreamed of, what I'd planned.

My face fell. *Did I have plans? Dreams?* As much as I liked to think so, freedom wasn't a gift often given to girls. I'd heard that in some places in the world, women weren't even allowed to speak unless their men gave them permission. *How prehistoric. They'd have to cut my tongue out.* I subconsciously ran my tongue across the back of my teeth and shuddered.

Drystan sensed my dimming mood and hustled off with the snails.

I picked a kitchen knife off the bench that sat beside the empty buckets from yesterday's catch. We'd been digging snails for a week, and still, the flats were full of the beasts. Local legend tells that they grew from the dirt like the undead, but instead of fangs and claws, they used slime as their weapon.

Twirling the blade between my fingers to calm myself, I stared into the hearth at the room's center, the flames more than happy to share their warmth as they danced.

All this bustle, all these people. They'd turned Town Hall into a preparation room. Hauled in everything needed to bake, broil, sew, and clean—and I'm sure they hated every moment of it. Because of me, Lians would soon have a new overlord. If only I'd been born a boy, then this would be someone else's problem.

Sniffing along the edge of the bench, a bony mouse crept toward the remaining snails, hoping to steal a meal.

I smiled at it. So sweet, so soft—just like the prince would be, according to the other girls in the village. Every time they saw me, they sniggered behind their hands. An oversized wolverine of a woman, they called me. It's not that I'm ugly, per se, but I stood as tall—if not taller—than most men and nearly as strong from the farm work I'd done since I could walk. In a gown, I'd be a laughingstock.

I flicked my wrist, and the knife soared, lodging into the mouse's neck—just as Drystan returned for more buckets. He yelped, "Lord above, Rhia!"

I yanked the blade out of the floorboard, picking up the mouse by its tail. *I know someone that needs a hot meal.* I gestured to the last of the buckets. "Get the rest of them into the wagon, then meet me outside. Hurry, before Mama and Papa come back."

Drystan rolled his eyes. "So bossy, and you're not even a princess yet. Give me a second."

I just dipped my chin in response, hoping he didn't see how much that comment unsettled me—princess. *I'd rather be a cavern hag . . . or a spinster. Who am I kidding? They're the same thing.*

By the time we'd hiked home together, the rain had returned. First in a heavy mist, but it wasn't long before it became a full-blown downpour. The mud deepened the further from the town's center we walked, filling my boots and seeping between my toes.

Our hut was small—much too small to house four people. With only two rooms, we used one as a combined kitchen and dining area, and the other a bedroom we all shared, sleeping on separate straw mats.

Dripping wet, I peeled off my coat as I stepped inside, laying it over the back of our rickety wooden chair. My cheeks burned from the cold, and I patted them, hoping to get some sensation back into my fingers and face. Drystan wasn't far behind.

I wandered into our bedroom, and as expected, my fat orange tabby—Jacc—lay sprawled over my mat.

"Jaccy," I whispered in a sing-song voice, and he raised his head, whiskers rumpled from sleep. I dangled the mouse and *whap*—he clawed it from my fingers and hunched over the rodent, growling and spitting as if he'd caught the wretched thing himself. Gently, I stroked his back, careful not to bump his stiff, aging hindlegs.

Drystan leaned against the doorway, water dripping from his coat as heavily as it leaked through the holes in the roof. "We're not going to have enough food to last the winter, you know. Especially not after this feast."

I nodded slowly, ruffling Jacc's fur.

"Maybe this prince can help."

I snorted. "Well, if worse comes to worst, we can just eat him, I guess. Great idea."

Drystan chuckled softly, then patted my shoulder. "Everything is going to be okay."

I smirked. "You can marry him, then, if you're so sure."

"Rhia," He exhaled, shaking his head as he walked away. From the sound of it, to stoke the coals in the fire. Jacc smeared the mouse's blood on my pants as he crawled onto my lap. I kissed his soft head as he licked his paws clean.

If only I could stay here forever. Freeze this moment in time, so my future would never come, it fading away like a nightmare by dawn. By tomorrow night, I would no longer be Rhiannon Caddell, the mayor's daughter. The wild child—flying as free as a dandelion seed on a summer breeze.

I would be a princess—a prince's *wife,* and never had a thought disturbed me more.

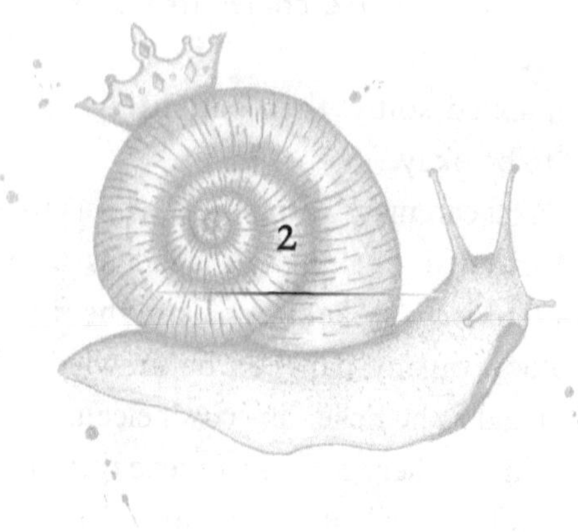

2

"Fowl are not fortune tellers."

Cheep, chirp, cheep.

I scrunched my eyes, pulling my worn blanket over my head.

Cheep, chirp.

"WAKE UP!"

I screeched as the morning sun blasted through my cracked window.

"Wake up, Rhia, do you hear the birdsong?" Mama jerked open the curtains as she danced into the room, pressed blue skirts twirling around her, matching her high-necked plaid bodice, thick brown hair braided tightly around her head like a crown. Dust fairies swirled around her as if summoned by her musical voice and *not* by the fact that I hadn't swept in months.

Time could kiss her bum, Mama would always be beautiful. The lines around her eyes and mouth—born of laughter—

couldn't hurt her beauty, only enhance it. *Will I age so well, or will I be one of those crones with chin hairs the length of a green onion?*

The more important question, though, is had she waited outside the bedroom for just this brief moment of sunshine? It wouldn't surprise me. Mama has always been a bit dramatic, Papa said. Drystan called her quirks the lunacies of a madwoman.

Scowling, I blinked away the remaining sleep clogging my senses and repeated. "Birdsong?"

Mama beamed, hands clasped over her chest, and sighed. "Your special day has been blessed. I remember waking up on my wedding day to a chorus of woodlarks and nightingales."

My brows furrowed. "I thought you said it hailed at your wedding."

Mama blew out a breath. "Yes, yes, but the birds still sang." Her expression softened then, round and loving. "You know, this is a blessing in disguise."

"Sure," I sat up, back popping. What I wouldn't give to be taken out and beaten like a dirty rug. "For you and Papa, maybe —but sorry to say, I don't think I'm enough of a prize to persuade the prince to forgive Lians' debt or Papa's attitude. You're better off putting Drystan in a dress."

Mama glowered. I shouldn't have said that. Words cut deep. "You know it's not like that."

"Of course, it's not." I rose, standing a good six inches taller than her. "I'm sure his highness will love having me to look up to."

Recovering, Mama gave me a coy smile and tugged on the too-short hem of my nightgown. "I'm sure he will. Don't they all? Get dressed. It's time to head to the castle."

Sighing, I hugged her before turning to shrug on the same dirty clothes I wore yesterday. It's not like I needed to impress anyone.

———

Ah, the castle.

A giant, hulking, stone monstrosity. Chunks of rock lay missing from the tall, rounded towers, along with half the parapet. An unintentional moat had formed around the structure's base with the recent rain, but at least the bridge was still intact—even if the portcullis hung rusted on its hinges. High up on a hill, the west side of the castle looked over the Wentwood, burning oranges and golds with late autumn approaching. The east stood over the open fields and meadows that eventually joined to the region's main road, sprinkled with wild daffodils and spotted orchids in the spring, barely visible over the endless, bright lavender blossoms. If I could bottle the divine fragrance for you, I would.

I sat at the head of the wagon, alongside Papa, as he drove the horses through the gates and into the castle's inner courtyard. I glanced around as he pulled to a stop, taking in the deterioration.

I hadn't been here in years. The bilberry bushes, filled with bright blue fruit, had overtaken the stairwells leading to the castle's upper levels. Weeds grew between the bricks, now streaked with algae and mud. I exhaled, plucking a berry of the nearest bush. "The prince will be so pleased. He has only to step out his front door to find a full breakfast. No cooks required."

Papa stepped off the carriage, giving me an apologetic look as he helped me down. "We'll get things fixed up, I promise. We just ran out of time."

"Oh, no," I drawled, waving flippantly. "It's perfect. Showcases the state of our future flawlessly, don't you think?"

Papa's lips drooped. "We're not doing this to punish you."

"So I've heard." I started for the nearest staircase. I just wanted to be alone. I couldn't take any more of these empty promises, or words of encouragement while the speaker's eyes showed only doubt and pity. It reminded me of how Mama looked when she swore the medicinal tea she tried to feed us tasted like candy.

A bilberry bush caught the laces of my boot—I yelped—and a moment later, my face hit the stone. A star-flecked pain shot through my jaw. "Fart in a jam jar—" I cursed, spitting blood where I bit my lip, the metallic tang coating my tongue. I could already feel a bruise forming.

Behind me, I heard Drystan's full-bodied laugh. I shot a glare over my shoulder just as he trotted into the courtyard on his bay mare. Jealousy licked at my ankles. Our family horses belonged to him, Mama, and Papa. Our last broodmare died before she could foal my mount. I would never forgive Drystan for being two minutes older and getting her last colt.

Drystan tried to hold back his grin as I got to my feet, but he did a poor job of it. Instead, he bowed in his saddle, sniggering. "The picture of grace and elegance, your highness."

We swapped rude gestures.

"Enough of that." Appearing on the top of the stairwell, Mama pulled me up by my collar. Tsking, she grabbed my chin, checking either side of my face. "Lord above, you chose today of all days to have an accident? You're no better than a newborn grasshopper."

I smirked. "Just trying to keep you on your toes."

Mama scoffed, dragging me the rest of the way up the stairs. I looked back, mouthing cries for help, and Drystan saluted me. Papa's attention remained a little too focused on the wagon, his cheeks red. He couldn't save me from Mama's preening, and he knew it.

Despite my throbbing jaw, now that we were inside, I was glad to see that the halls were dry and well-lit, even with the castle's poor condition. The entire village spent weeks sweeping and scrubbing every level—along with sewing new bedding for the bed chambers so the prince's company wouldn't have to sleep in mouse droppings.

In my opinion, they should have left the droppings—good character building for the rich folk, don't you agree?

Beyond the entrance hall, the castle's keep held a fairly standard dining hall, adorned with a raised dais for the lords to sit. Crushed red velvet hung on the walls coated with dust, along with tapestries displaying the history of Lians—a fascinating tale of potatoes and snails. Long tables ran in rows through the hall's lengths, creating an aisle that ran up the center for the wedding party to walk during the ceremony.

I shook my head and swallowed, throat dry. *Not now, Rhia, don't panic. You still have a few hours.*

Each tower had a suite on its upper level, with the lower levels used to house private libraries, kitchens, armories, and medical wings. Papa took me on several tours of the castle when I was younger. We'd ride up the steep, narrow road from the village, looking up to the towers, and I'd wonder why they were here in the first place.

Gwent had never had a prince, at least from the records I could find. Lians, in particular—had always ruled itself. I sometimes wondered if that was our downfall. I doubted these people—my people—would ever accept a leader besides my father. The role of mayor would pass to Drystan one day, but I would out-rank him now. Even as one of their own, I didn't know if Lians would follow me . . . a woman, and traitor now that I would be technically a part of the royal family.

After weaving through a maze of corridors and climbing what felt like an endless number of stairs, Mama squealed as she opened the door to the North tower's suite. "Here we are!"

I stepped inside my room—anxious—and found the chamber to be precisely what I'd expected—cozy but boring as a dried-out cow patty. Is it odd I felt . . . relieved?

On the far wall, a large-shuttered window lay open, letting

in the soft autumn light. A wide bed—a real bed, with a feather mattress—sat to the left, covered by a canopy. In a separate adjoined room, a copper tub sat filled to the brim with steaming water. Back in the bedroom, jewelry and pins lay strewn over a vanity. Some of the jewels I recognized as belonging to women in the village.

I tried to swallow down the lump forming in my throat. How much had they sacrificed for me?

"Well," Mama clapped her hands together. "Better jump in while the water is still warm."

I shrugged off my coat. "Who hauled all this up here?"

Mama smiled, tense. "Your brother. Some of the other men helped with the water."

Nodding, I stepped out of my clothes and into the tub, startling at the heat against my bare thighs. As Mama scrubbed my hip-length blonde hair, I stared at my reflection in the standing mirror across from the tub—stared at my square face, covered in freckles. At my large but hooded eyes. Not ugly, but not royalty. My skin was too dark from years in the fields. My frame too broad. Not the slight, shapely figure I'm sure the prince expected. I slumped against the rim of the tub.

"He's going to love you," Mama whispered.

I blinked at my reflection, at hers behind me. "And if he doesn't?"

"Then he'll respect you. And you'll make him."

She tapped my shoulder a short time later, and I rose from the tub, wrapping myself in a fluffy robe. Midway through drying my hair, I realized Mama still watched me. I faced her, brows raised, and her throat bobbed.

"Things . . ." She hesitated. "Will be expected of you tonight."

I froze, eyes wide. *Dear, Lord, no.* "We don't need to talk about that."

Mama wrung her hands. "It can be very . . . painful, the first time."

"We *really* don't need to talk about this."

Mama exhaled sharply. "All I'm saying is . . . all I want to say is . . . don't be afraid to say no."

I forced a smile. *Please stop.* "Thank you."

"And if he doesn't back off, don't be afraid to kick him in the—"

"*Thank you*, Mama." I cringed and sat at the vanity. "I'll remember."

Mama nodded, smiling weakly. She grabbed a comb and started ripping through my tangled mane. I tried to hide my winces as she hit snag after snag. After nearly scalping me, she braided the top section into an intricate swirl, the bottom left loose and wavy. Mama slipped a silver comb above the braids and stepped back, beaming. "You look beautiful."

I scoffed. "Oh yes, pearls on a pig."

Mama swatted my arm. "Hush. Besides, I've spent all this time making you the perfect dress."

I held in a gasp. I hadn't thought she'd *make* me a dress. I assumed I'd squeeze into hers or borrow one from one of the other women.

Mama pulled a lengthy box from under the vanity and laid it on the bed. She gestured me to open it, and I hated the excitement lacing through my fingers. I ran my nails along the lid, letting them catch on the seam, holding my breath. Mama made me a dress. She made me a—

I opened the package.

Inside lay the most ungodly, matronly hunk of off-white lace I'd ever seen.

I lifted it, holding the monstrosity against my body as I turned to the mirror. The length only came to my ankles—an appalling and inappropriate aspect in itself—the skirt poofing out into an oval bell shape. Red and green ribbon crisscrossed the bodice, the neckline tickling my chin with ruffled lace. The sleeves were snug, except for the wrists, elbows, and shoulders, where they created more horrific poofs.

Breathing heavily, I slipped it on, and Mama laced it up—of course, it fit like a glove. But my frame in this fabric . . .

I looked up, tears filling my eyes. "Mama, it's—"

"Ghastly?" Mama squawked out a laugh, eyes crinkling. "Appalling?"

I sucked on my lips.

"I was worried you wouldn't like it, but after what you did with the snails . . . " Mama cocked her head and smiled. "I think I made the right choice."

I fought against my smile. "You saw that?"

She waved a hand in front of her nose. "Child, I smelled that when they started the stew. I knew who was behind it."

I turned back to the mirror. Besides my face, filled with color, I looked genuinely atrocious. I wrapped Mama in a tight hug. "It's absolutely hideous. I love it."

Mama squeezed me even tighter. "I knew you would." She stepped back and wiped at her weepy eyes. "Stay here, rest. I'll go make sure the preparations are coming along as they should."

I nodded. Neither of us were one for unnecessary words. After she left, I slipped off the dress, put it back in its package, then shrugged back into my robe. The ceremony was still hours away. My family would "kidnap" me in a traditional wedding, and the groom's party would come to my rescue. A valiant knight swooping the distressed damsel into his arms before they rode off into the sunset.

But Papa put a stop to that. *I refuse to have court toads galloping all over my property like fools, tearing up my grass.* Even so, I would still have to wait.

Mama hadn't been gone half an hour when the shouting started outside, along with the sharp click of hooves on stone. I padded to the window, a rush of adrenaline making my legs shake. Leaning over the sill, I shielded my eyes from the sun glare on the cobblestone below.

A tacky carriage sat in the courtyard—thrice the size of my family's wagon. A sleek black box adorned with gold roses and silver thorns—ridiculous. The decorations alone could feed Lians for ten years. Three more smaller carriages pulled in behind.

My lips twitched into a smile. *Maybe once we're married, I'll strip it and sell it for parts.*

Papa stood beside the main carriage, speaking to its driver, who then passed the horses' reins to Drystan. The driver stepped down and opened the carriage door.

I held my breath. *Here we go. This is it.*

Knowing my luck, I'd be spending the rest of my life in the bed of a pale, spongy troll. You can imagine my confusion when an older woman stepped out instead.

As I expected, she dressed well—wearing a matronly black gown embroidered in the same golds and silvers, a matching scarf covering her greying hair. *She looks like she's in mourning.* A giggle escaped my lips. *Aren't we all?*

I cringed as Papa kissed her knobby fingers, gesturing toward the castle, showing what was likely to be her new home. Next out the carriage was a younger girl, about my age, also dressed in the same colors. A petite, pretty, little thing. Her corset as absurdly tight as her coif was tall. My stomach clenched. *Who is she to the prince?* The girl moved to stand beside the older woman, and I didn't miss the way Drystan's eyes followed her.

Men.

Finally, a pale face emerged from the carriage. Pale—I got that prediction correct—from never doing a day's work in his life, I imagined.

Emerys Beyron—Prince of Wales, and the King's sixth son, exited the carriage.

Papa—and even Drystan—bowed.

It appalled me that my first thought was that *at least he's not ugly.*

Now, I was *annoyed* by his raw good looks—creamy skin, black-brown hair, perfect jawline and cheekbones. Body long and lean, but not frail. *I should have known—another tool in his manipulative arsenal.* The prince waved his hand, allowing my father and brother to rise. If I'd been in range, I would have beat him using his pretty toothpick companion as a club.

Serve. That's what the gesture commanded—the expectation of Lians from now on.

What would be expected of me.

Papa gestured for the prince to follow, and his royal highness was halfway up the stairs before he froze. Turning, he looked up—large, ice-blue eyes locking onto mine—and smiled, almost nervously. Even the shade of his irises were more extravagant than my dark, steely blue.

My innards turned to liquid. I slammed the window shut, right onto my fingers, and cursed. Too loudly.

A low chuckle rose from the courtyard. If it were possible to die of embarrassment, I would have croaked right then and there.

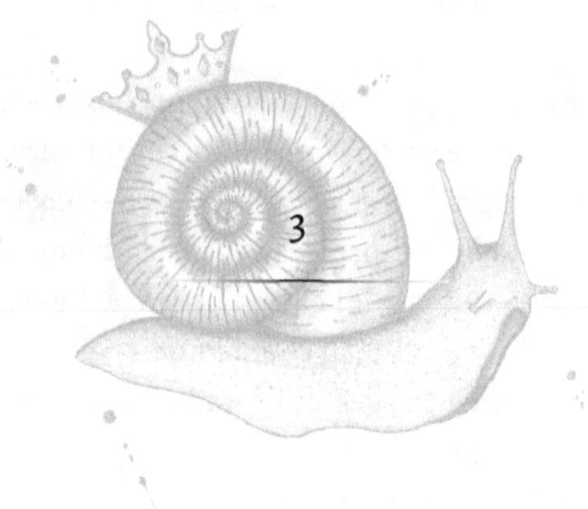

3

"A union of oil and sewage."

Hours later, I still waited for the ceremony to start—curse Mama's compulsive need for punctuality.

I watched the trickle of light leaking through the window as it made its slow climb across the chamber floor, crack by crack, taunting me. I'd considered napping—the bed looked comfortable—but couldn't relax long enough to fall asleep, especially with the looming fear of ruining my hair.

Perhaps after seeing me in the window, the prince changed his mind. I'm sure I'd looked pathetic—as if gawking, instead of trying to scope out the enemy. If not me, then one glance at the castle would send him packing back to his father.

The King.

The man who could decide the fate of an entire people he'd never met or cared for if I couldn't convince his son otherwise.

I exhaled completely. *One step at a time.* If I survived tonight,

I'd worry about the rest. I didn't know if the prince's pretty face lessened the dread of my wifely duties or made it worse. *One step at a time.*

The *thunk-thunk* of Papa's pegleg echoed down the hall, stopping outside my door before he knocked.

I cleared my throat, as dry as last summer's firewood. "Come in."

Papa's balding head peeked in, cheeks red, but otherwise, he seemed calm. Hopefully, that was a good sign. I stood, smoothing my dress as he stepped inside, holding his arms wide. "Rhi-Rhi, you look beautiful."

Silence.

We both let out a howling laugh. Papa wiped his eyes, extending his hand. "It's time."

My heart crashed into my stomach as I took his arm. Goosebumps skipped up my skin as we stepped into the hall. The candles in the sconces had burned low. They'd need replacement before long.

Deep breaths, deep breaths.

My eyes flitted to every crack and scuff on the floor, the cobwebs still hanging high up on the ceiling. What would this prince think of us? I would never say anything to Papa—he and the others worked so hard—but was it enough? How could I convince a man, used to the finest the world could offer, that *my world* was worth saving?

The cool, night air breezed around my ankles, chilling the floor beneath my beaded decorative slippers. Every second, every step we took toward the dining hall saw to my quickening pulse. My legs turned to lead, the ache in my shoulders unbearable. By the time we stopped outside the hall's wide, oak double doors, the only thing I could hear was the blood pounding in my ears.

An old, yet ornate, stool sat beside the doors. Papa lifted my bouquet off of it, handing it to me. I forced myself to smile, stroking the fresh myrtle leaves, their soft white flowers in full bloom. Such beauty. Such wonderful traditions. Would they all be lost once the prince took over?

Papa's grip on my arm tightened, tears welling in his eyes. "Are you ready?"

I smiled sweetly. "No."

A belly-aching laugh. "Me either." Papa's expression turned serious, and he shifted my hair forward to hide my bruised jaw. "I know what I said before, but we *are* counting on you."

My eyes narrowed. *I knew it.*

Papa seemed so sad, but his pouting did nothing to lessen my hurt. "Lians is counting on you. Don't let us down."

With all the rage burning through my blood, I could have just walked away—right then and there—but instead, I nodded, letting the anger ripple off my skin. Let the prince have me and his dowry of snails and mud. I wouldn't weep, not for him. "Let's get this over with."

Papa flinched at the sharpness of my tone as he flung open the doors.

A blast of light blinded me. I blinked, adjusting. Fixed on me were over one hundred sets of eyes. Frantic, I searched for a friendly face and found Mama and Drystan standing beside the dais.

The aisle—the path split up the center of the room, separating the prince's small group from mine. A girl from the village—the blacksmith's young daughter—waited by the door with a pail of white flowers.

I allowed myself to look at who stood beside her, waiting for me, and my breaths became too shallow.

Prince Emerys Beyron.

His dark hair—so typical of the country's Western half—fell in glistening waves to his ears and across his forehead.

And those pale eyes were so . . . so . . .

Completely and utterly bored.

Lifeless—his expression remained blank, even at the sight of my gown and bruise. He just stood there in his stupid black doublet and matching cape. You'd think he'd been waiting for a council meeting to be over instead of attending his own wedding. He pursed his full lips as he offered me his arm, where he'd then walk me to the dais.

I could do it—punch him in his straight, perfect nose.

Papa tugged me forward, attempting grace despite the limp his leg gave him. He muttered, "Easy." He must have felt my tension. I forced my body to relax.

I've got to be better than him. I slapped on an equally indifferent expression as I looped elbows with the prince, his arm as rigid as his demeanor. A priest stood atop the dais across the room—he wasn't from Lians. His over-the-top gold and red robes looked so out of place in the castle's worn-down interior. Lines of candles sat lit along the aisle, flickering, watching, waiting to set my gown on fire.

Papa bowed as he offered me to my suitor—an acceptance of the marriage. The prince smiled, though it didn't reach his eyes, and lengthened his arm to grip my hand. I accepted it without looking at him, noticing the smoothness of his skin. Too soft— not callused like Papa's or my brother's.

Dear God, those blathering girls were right. I couldn't help but wonder if other parts of him were soft too, but I shook my head to chase the thought away. *Bad, bad, bad.*

The prince gave me a concerned look, the first emotion I'd seen from him.

I tried to ignore the heat building in my cheeks, keeping my focus on the priest and his altar. Music began to blare, slightly off tune, and the flower girl started her trek down the aisle. She dropped handfuls of petals in thick clumps every few paces. The prince and I followed in step, trying unsuccessfully to match each other's strides. Though his grip was light, the tension radiating through his fingers traveled up my arm, making my jaw stiffen.

Please, Lord, let this end. Let me survive.

I felt like a thousand years before the flower girl dumped the last of her petals on my feet, darting into the sidelines to my right. Caddic—the blacksmith lifted her into his arms, winking as he caught my eye. The prince's hand tightened around mine, and when I looked, he was scowling at Caddic. His eyes flickered to mine, and I looked away, heat crawling back into my cheeks. *Lord, scratch that, please—just end me now.*

The music died out as the prince and I managed to step onto the dais. The priest jerked me to the left, and I stumbled as my ankle rolled. A few giggles burst from the crowd. If I hadn't been so irritated and in pain, I would have died of embarrassment yet again.

Somehow, I kept my hands steady as the priest rested the prince's over mine, wrapping a golden ribbon around our wrists, weaving it between our fingers as he recited a cordial speech. *Forget formalities, I guess. He wants this over with as much as I do.* He pulled two small silk boxes out of his robes—our rings.

As hard as I tried not to, I found myself peeking at the prince's face again, only to be surprised to see him watching me, almost curiously.

I rose a brow at him in question. At least he was only about two inches shorter than me, at most, unlike most of the men in the village. Maybe, they were small from a poor diet. He arched a well-groomed brow back, the priest's voice booming, and whispered. "What's your name?"

My stomach knotted. *They didn't even tell him my name.* Maybe the King hadn't known. Most likely, he hadn't cared. I opened my mouth to answer, but my words were drowned by the priest, beating me to the punch. "Do you, Rhiannon Caddell, take Prince Emerys Beyron, an heir of Wales, to be your lawfully wedded husband?"

Here it was—the catalyst of my doom—but I wouldn't go down easily. I wasn't a bleating damsel, weeping over ripped stitches. I'd brought thousand-pound horses to their knees for giving me a sour look, more than once. I'd castrated sheep and steers—I wasn't afraid of a one-hundred and fifty-pound man. I shot the prince a wicked smile and crooned, taking his modest silver ring from its box and sliding it over his third finger. "I do. I give you that which is mine to give."

His full lips twitched up at the corners. Did I just see a flicker of amusement?

The priest spoke again. "Do you, Prince Emerys Beyron, an heir of Wales, take Rhiannon Caddell to be your lawfully wedded wife?"

Any emotion I might have seen from the prince disappeared, replaced again with that boredom. From the second box, he pulled an even simpler gold band. I'd expected some absurdly large stone, but the gold . . . it looked rich against my tanned skin as he slid it onto my finger. "I do. I give you that which is mine to give."

The priest slammed his Bible shut. "I now pronounce you husband and wife. You may now kiss the bride."

Oh no.

Oh *no.*

Time stopped. I'd forgotten this part. If our hands weren't bound together, I would have bolted. I must have looked as horrified as I felt because the prince flashed me an apologetic smile. My heart nearly cracked through my sternum as he leaned in, pressing a quick, thoughtless kiss to the corner of my mouth—no time for me to run.

Before I knew it, we faced a cheering crowd, but I didn't miss the tense edge on my people's faces or their half-hearted claps. The prince raised our hands in victory, and as everyone stood, lining up to pay their respects. You'd think they were heading to the chopping block—so sullen and dragging.

The older woman from the carriage approached the dais first, wrapping her ribbon around our wrists. I couldn't help comparing her face to a puckered cat's anus. She beamed at the prince, but I saw the sadness in her beady eyes. Before she stepped down, she shot me a scathing glare, which I instinctually matched. I wasn't in the mood for bad attitudes.

Papa replaced her. He spurted off some practiced happy words as he tied on his ribbon, carefully avoiding my eye. Mama came next, then Drystan, then the pretty girl that had arrived with the prince. One by one, the villagers and the prince's company followed suit, not bothering with congratulations. They just tied their ribbons and left.

With every person that approached, the prince's posture grew stiffer and stiffer. I finally gave him a questioning look, irritation building. Catching my eye, he cleared his throat, inclining his chin toward me. "You'd think they'd be more uplifted by the prospect of a cooperative union."

Narrowing my eyes, I snapped. "In my experience, cooperation does little to ward off hunger pangs and fleas."

Prince Emerys' throat bobbed, and he gave me—dare I say— an appraising look. "Well said, my lady."

I bristled. "You mock me?"

He blinked. "No, no, not at all, I—"

The priest cut in front of us, raising his hands. "As this ceremony concludes, let the reception begin. Ladies?"

Several of the younger women in the crowd burst into giggles, whispering to one another.

Oh yes, the pin toss—a silly tradition that never failed to create a desperate man-hunter in the village, seeking to rope down the husband her catch promised her. I'd heard most countries threw their bouquets, but that seemed wasteful to me, especially when the myrtle could be planted in the garden for the next wedding.

The girls rushed to the center of the hall while the tables

were dragged away, tripping over their gowns. Pink cheeked and giddy, wide grins stared up at me.

I tried to smile back, but I think it came out as more of a grimace. Perhaps being married wasn't so bad. I'd never have to partake in this horrible event again. The last time, I ended up giving a girl a bloody nose—my taken opportunity to punch one of those dumb ninnies and make it look like an accident.

Somehow, the prince and I managed to turn together, our backs to the crowd.

Let's get this over with. Carefully, I undid the small silver broach pinned to my chest—silver, because my family couldn't afford ceremonial gemstones. I rubbed it between my thumb and forefinger. *The same pin Mama wore. She turned out okay.*

With a deep breath, I closed my eyes and hucked it over my shoulder. Even facing away, I could picture the pin's descent by the scaling intensity of the women's gasps.

I twisted, just in time to see the first thrown punch.

A city girl hit the ground as a blow from a village girl stuck her in the jaw. She screamed, launching on her attacker, who stood braced and ready. Now, they rolled on the ground in front of the dais, legs in the air, screeching as they yanked each other's hair.

The horror on the prince's face gave me more pleasure than I'd felt in weeks.

An angry shout in the crowd made me look up. A village woman pointed to a slim figure standing away from the brawl— the prince's pretty carriage companion—silver pin cradled in her delicate cupped hands. Eyes wide, she backed away slowly, as if expecting the mob to turn on her like hungry wolves.

And they might have—they looked ferocious enough—but thankfully, the priest intervened. Flashing a cheesy smile, he wrapped his arm around her shoulders, guiding her toward the dais as he addressed the men in the hall. "Any takers? Anyone? This one is a beauty."

Drystan scowled as the boys took their turns hooting and howling.

As tradition expected, the prince and I each kissed her cheek, declaring the "winner." She gave me a hesitant smile, hair smelling of mint, as I embraced her. *For her sake, I hope she has a knife tucked under those skirts.*

The entire hall gave her a round of applause. As soon as the poor girl sat, she was surrounded by potential suitors vying for her attention.

"That was . . . " The prince hesitated. "An experience."

I smirked. "Not your idea of a good time?"

He gave me a mischievous look. It looked nice on him. "Is it yours?"

Some feeling made my lower stomach tighten as I said. "You'll find out soon enough."

As if on cue, the music began again. Not a procession this time, but a faster melody—an invitation to begin our first dance. My throat tightened to near suffocating with terror. I could wrangle large animals, but dance? I'd rather cut off my toes.

The tune seemed to have the opposite effect on the prince. His shoulders relaxed, and he gave me a small smile as he bowed and said, "Care to dance?"

Atop the dais . . . where everyone could see.

No, no, no, no, no, no. I forced my lips to smile back, only because Mama and Papa were watching. "If it pleases you."

He dipped his chin, reaching out to clasp my elbow—a movement I mirrored. It took every ounce of my focus not to trip over my feet or his as we leapt into a spiraling prance. A cheer went up, and the crowd split into two groups—one on each side of the hall. Each group joined hands, bouncing to the music—coming together then apart with the opposite party in a steady rhythm, stealing each other's partners, laughing, and enjoying themselves.

How long that lasted, I didn't know. The prince's steps were practiced and light, even as the pace quickened. Faster and faster, we twirled, sweat beading on our temples. So entranced with our dance, I didn't notice when he'd leaned in close enough to whisper. "You're better at this than I expected."

I froze, dead in my tracks.

The prince nearly slammed into my side, catching himself on my shoulder. His eyes wide, I straightened, holding his gaze, and spat. "I'm sorry, did you expect a toothless nag?"

The prince blinked once, twice, stunned. "I never said—"

Insufferable pig. Trying to keep the upper hand, I moved to step off the dais—completely forgetting our adjoined wrists. I fell from the first step in slow motion, waiting for my face to collide into the second when the prince's free arm wrapped around my waist.

The crowd paused—sucking in a universal breath—then continued as if nothing happened when they realized I wasn't about to die.

My and the prince's eyes met, just for a moment, and I saw in that icy gaze what I can only describe as desperate hope. I hissed. "Don't touch me."

The prince's face fell.

"It's time for the feast!" The priest darted in, smoothing his robes. "Let us move to our tables and catch our breath."

Entire body on fire, I swatted the prince's hand away, smoothing my hair over my shoulder as I made to join the others. The prince cleared his throat, gesturing behind us. I followed his gaze.

Lord Almighty—I hadn't even noticed the separate dining table they'd set for us on the dais. The prince smiled weakly. "Shall we?"

I could feel the eyes boring into us from below.

I held his stare, breathing heavily. *Tradition can find the back-*

door. I yanked my hand free of our bindings, still breathless from our dance, and swept past him to our table, chin high.

No one said a word.

And no one would—not unless they wanted me to cut their throats with a rusty spoon.

4

"Foiled plans and wrinkled adversaries."

With my abnormally stretched frame, awkwardness was a familiar guest to me in social situations.

For the prince, well—not so much.

As the village girls served the main course, The prince shifted in his chair six times, picking at his already immaculate nails. Was it normal for a man to have such clean hands? I'd never seen anything like it. Even on bathing days, I could never get all the grit out from beneath my cuticles, let alone every ounce of oil out of my hair. Yet, his locks still lay in flawless waves despite the sweat we'd built in our dance.

As supper was wheeled in, an overwhelming stench spread through the hall, breaking through the perfumes emitting from the prince's skin. Beside him, I twirled my fork, trying to contain my smile as servers passed around heaping bowls of stew.

Terrible as it is to say, it didn't bother me one bit that my people would be ingesting those filthy creatures along with the prince. When Papa announced the marriage, none of them came to my rescue. Not even Caddic, the blacksmith. Who more than once expressed interest in what lay hidden beneath my skirts. Not that I'd ever give it to him—or any other man. Nor would I, but it still stung.

They placed my and the prince's stew on our table, set aside on a covered platter. Even still, I could smell the mud and earth seeping out from beneath the lid. The prince ran his fingertip along the edge of his empty bowl. Instead of giving the command for supper to be served, the prince whispered, almost to himself. "Rhiannon."

I grit my teeth, impatient. "Yes?"

"Rhiannon," He repeated thoughtfully. "Named for the Great Queen?"

"Perhaps." I shrugged. "Or perhaps my parents just liked the name."

Prince Emerys rapped his nails on the side of his goblet, eyes bright. "It's said the Great Queen was a healer. That the songs of the birds that served her could raise the dead or lull the living to sleep."

I snorted. "You're a romantic?"

"Is that bad quality?"

"Depends." Another shrug. "My songs make the dead praise being below the ground, and the living beg to be down with them."

The prince began to laugh—a musical sound—but the priest appeared behind us, raising his arms in a flourishing motion. What kind of weddings did they have in the royal cities to turn their Holy men into braying goats? His over-inflated ego made me want to dunk him into a water trough.

"As custom demands, the bride must present the groom their first meal as man and wife." The priest nodded to me. "You may proceed, princess."

I looked up. A hall of grumpy, hungry faces stared at us, waiting. I'd forgotten the guests couldn't eat until we'd begun. Trying to keep the guilt off my face, I stood.

Though we referred to it as snail stew, the meal was named *cawl*—a classic Welsh dish, usually served with lamb or beef chunks, but in Lians, we had snails. Lots of them. I'd spent years digging through the mud collecting them because the creatures were all the nourishment we had.

I plastered on my biggest, toothiest smile as I took the covered bowl from the tray and set it in front of my blessed husband. Who, I'm sure, had never felt the pangs of true hunger —never knew what it's like to spend days in the forest, only to come home to the hungry faces in your charge, empty-handed. I'd seen the despair on Papa's face, more than once, when he had nothing to give to our starving neighbors but the food off *our* plates. I'm sure I'd see the look again before the coming winter passed.

Spoons clanked as the guests prepared to dig in. As I uncovered the prince's dish, I noticed a pair of eyes watching me from the crowd—the older woman. She held a small blade, cutting into a round hunk of wood, leaving shavings all over the table. Where did she get the wood? Did her headscarf have pockets? As I caught her gaze, her beady watery eyes narrowed.

I sense an arch nemesis in the making. I looked away sharply, guts churning. The prince glanced from his stew to me, grimacing, no doubt at the smell. Lord, I enjoyed watching him squirm. Smiling, I ran my fingertips along the edge of his bowl seductively and breathed. "Enjoy."

Throat bobbing, still holding a smile, the prince took the smallest spoonful possible while the entire crowd watched, his utensil coming back adorned with a considerably sized snail. I bite back the giggles building in my throat as the spoon passed his lips. His eyes widened as he chewed and swallowed. Instead of projectile vomiting—like I'd hoped—the prince's entire body relaxed.

And in turn, the entire hall relaxed. He took a larger spoonful and chewed it happily.

I stared at him blankly. *This must be a joke.*

The prince gave me an almost guilty smile. Maybe he felt bad for doubting me. "This is superb, thank you."

I meant to smile back, but I may have bared my teeth instead. Plopping down in my seat, I sipped my wine as the crowd began to eat. The prince's entire party brightened as they tasted the stew—even the older woman.

They love it. Of all the terrible luck. Forget the birdsong—this marriage is cursed.

By the time they served the next course—rabbit rarebit—everyone had returned to enjoying themselves, becoming more boisterous as they pounded back drink after drink. The prince ate his meal in silence—as did I.

A selfish part of me wanted them to be miserable—not celebrating at my expense. It shouldn't bother me, but I couldn't shake the resentment. What *should* matter is that they were happy, even if only for as long as this evening lasted.

Once the berry cakes hit the table, the last of my resilience burnt out. It took four days for Drystan and me to pick enough berries for the desserts, and these upper-classers shoved them in their mouths like they'd be a daily indulgence. Even the wine was something we were only able to drink on *very* special occasions in the village. These powder-puffs chugged it down like water.

I couldn't stomach it.

I pushed back my chair, legs squeaking against the floor, and stood. The prince lifted his eyes from the table for the first time since supper began, giving me a concerned look.

I dipped my chin, feigning embarrassment. "I just have to . . .

you know." Like needing to pee should ever have to be embarrassing.

He nodded in response, as if it was normal to give someone permission to relieve themselves. No one seemed to notice as I rushed off the dais, heading toward the main doors leading into the hall. *Some fresh air, that's all I need.* Just to breathe for a minute, collect myself.

I nearly collided with the small, hunched figure that stepped into my path. "Oh, forgive me." I caught myself in the doorway, breathing in the scent of freshly cut pine. "I didn't mean to—"

"But you did mean it, didn't you?" The voice was low, grumbling—the older woman. Bits of her greying hair peeking out of the scarf around her head—no pockets in sight.

I froze. "Excuse me?"

The older woman's eyes were so dark they could scare the black off coal, and oh my, were they cunning. They narrowed into evil little slits. "You planned on humiliating our prince, didn't you? Blessed that you have such a wonderful chef to counteract your classless sense of humor."

I didn't miss the way she emphasized "our" prince. I puffed out my chest. "We don't have *chefs* here, but yes, my mother has an exceptional talent. And if class is a concern for you, I suggest a less gaudy color palette."

"Hmm." The older woman licked her narrow, cracked lips. "So, that's what this is about."

What does she mean by that? As I straightened my back, the top of her head came only to my breasts. "And who are you, may I ask?"

"I'm glad to hear that you can at least speak a proper sentence." She gave me a jerky curtsy, a noticeable pain plaguing her knees.

"Thank you. Again, my mother taught me."

"I'm sure she did." She straightened. "My name is Catrin. I started as the prince's caretaker. Now I serve as his advisor."

I chomped down on my lip to hold back a laugh. "*Our* prince takes advice from his nanny?"

Catrin's dangerous eyes flashed. "You would mock him?"

I fought the urge to step back. "No, but I question the . . . fortitude . . . of a man that would rely on *your* council. No offense."

Catrin's smile was something wicked. "You'll come to appreciate a man that heeds the words of the women in his life." She stepped closer, close enough that I could smell the snails on her breath. "And believe me when I say that your trite is not the best way to start a marriage."

I held Catrin's gaze. *Show no weakness.*

Instead of waiting for me to respond, Catrin hobbled back toward to party. I glanced back to the dais and found the prince watching us, face and body tense. I blew him a kiss before turning on my heels, storming into the hall.

An *interesting* way to start a marriage, indeed.

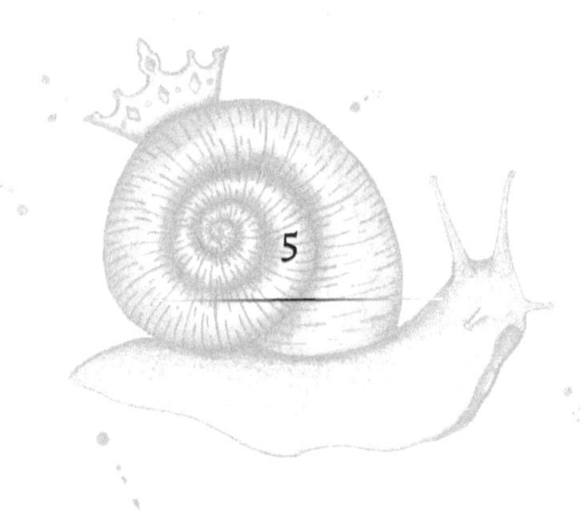

5

"A gauche meeting."

How long would it take the reception to notice I'd gone? Hopefully never. Then I could slip off into the night, never to be seen again—a lovely thought.

You've seen now, my distant friends, my precarious position. I'd like to tell you that my situation improves from here, but well, I'd be lying.

Stay tuned.

Frustrated tears streaked down my cheeks as I thundered down the hall toward my suite. Whether or not Catrin's harsh words or my failed plans caused my tears, I didn't know. Chills crawled up my limbs, my breath a heavy cloud. Without the warmth pouring from the dining hall's grand central hearth, pungently mixed with the heated press of dozens of sweating bodies around me, my teeth chattered against the frigid night air.

Who did that woman—Catrin—think she was? She didn't

know me or my circumstance, yet she'd throw accusations at my face? To be honest, that sounded like something I would do. How dare she use my own tactics against me.

Truthful accusations.

I *did* attempt to humiliate the prince, and she'd been the only one to notice. The only one bold enough to confront me. Those royal dung heaps invaded my home, took away my freedom. They should've expected retaliation . . . and should be grateful that all they got was tainted stew instead of an unexpected case of tragic death by poisoning. My lips twitched up at the corners. *Dear husband, may I interest you in the hemlock tartare? No? How about crème de la wolfsbane?*

All sounds of laughter and celebration died away by the time I reached the top of my private tower. The frigid air chilled my joints, causing them to ache, made all the worse by the excruciating climb. I pushed open my room's heavy oak doors, sending loud creak echoing down the spiral staircase behind me. I exhaled in relief as a blanket of warmth wrapped around my limbs. Someone had kept the fire going in my hearth—probably Mama.

Tall, leaking candles flickered on the window-sill and mantle, casting shadows over the faded blue furniture. I sunk into the sofa in front of the fire, wrapping my arms around my knees. Basking in the silence and solitude, I finally allowed my petty tears to shift into shuttering sobs—complete with mucus pouring from my nose like a breached dam.

I despised crying—a habit of the frail, in my opinion. I bet the prince's pretty friend cried all the time—sweet, perfect droplets that gracefully spilled from her long, thick lashes. But after weeks of anxious anticipation—not to mention the dread —of this day, it all poured out of me in ugly, racking sobs.

Never again could I slip out at the break of dawn and wander the forest for hours without hearing another's voice. The silent dawn and whispering dusk, a hushed creek followed by the patter of squirrel feet—all the ways the forest spoke without ever saying a word.

Now they would insist I had escorts or not allow me to leave at all. I wanted to run with Drystan and just be his sister—not his princess.

Never again could I just be me.

Either he didn't knock, or I didn't hear it over my gasping breaths. Though, I *did* hear as he cleared his throat, and I wheeled, slipper in hand—ready to use as a projectile weapon.

Prince Emerys ducked, standing in the cusp of my doorway, pale cheeks flushed, either from nerves or too much wine. I scanned his eyes, watching me warily, and found them to be crystal clear—definitely nerves. Probably caused by witnessing the blubbering mess that is his new wife.

"Should I—" He chewed the corner of his lip. "Should I come back later?"

I sniffed, wiping my dripping nose on the scratchy fabric of my sleeve. "Now? Later? What difference does it make?"

The prince's lips quirked—I guess I could call him Emerys now—and he closed the door behind him. Not a hair on his head sat out of place. Not one misplaced drop of stew stained his clothes. How irksome. *He's too perfect.* It tempted me to risk my chances soaring out the window as he approached. Instead, I sucked in a deep breath to compose myself. "Shouldn't you be entertaining your guests?"

He sat on the arm of the sofa, delicate as a flighty bird. Maybe he'd contemplated using the window himself. My nose burned as I wiped it a second time. *I must look horrid.* Prince Emerys had such a gentle voice—another ruse to trap me, as he said. "They're your guests, too, aren't they?"

I didn't know how to respond. Of course, they were my people, but neither they nor I wanted this marriage. I leaned back, folding my hands over my lap as I kept my gaze fixed on the coals in the fire. *Maybe if I ignore him, he'll go away.* I leaving the party was one thing, but you'd think the crowd would notice that their new ruler had disappeared.

After a few minutes of silence, he cleared his throat again. My eyes flashed in his direction. *Does he have allergies?*

"I realize," Emerys began. "That I haven't had a chance to introduce myself properly."

I snorted. "I know who you are."

A frown. "I'd still like the chance. It's only decent."

I turned on the sofa to face him, crossing my legs, then waved. "Then by all means, introduce yourself. I wait with bated breaths."

Emerys stood, lean body straight as an arrow, and smoothed his cape and tunic. He bowed, a practiced movement. "I am Emerys Beyron of Ceredigion, son of Berywn Beyron. It's a pleasure to make your acquaintance, my lady."

A giggle spilled out, and Emerys blinked up at me, scowling. Hand over my mouth, I sneered. "You think I'm a lady?"

Emerys cocked his head, still bent low. "Yes. Did you expect me to find you something different?"

"Don't lie. I'm a peasant." I matched his former scowl. "A dirty, farming peasant. Admit it."

Emerys straightened, expression thoughtful, then gave me a crooked smile. "You're not dirty."

"Cute." I shot back. I made sure he felt my contempt as he inched closer to the sofa. I leaned back into the cushions. "I met your crotchety friend this evening."

"I noticed." Emerys stiffened, pursing his lips. "And crotchety is a harsh word. I prefer to call her a gourmet cheese. Sharper with age, you know."

"And stinkier." I rested my chin on my knuckles. "You should serve her with crackers, then. She seems like joyful company."

"As does your beefy admirer." Emerys cocked his head. "A blacksmith by the look. The oversized right arm gives it away. Does the little girl's mother know he has an eye for you?"

I glared at him, hoping flames shot from my eyes. *Insufferable, royal trout.* I stood, pushing past him, and grabbed a pillow off the bed, yanking it out of its freshly sewn case. As I stuffed my old clothes into the sack, Emerys' brows furrowed in confusion. "What are you doing?"

I rolled my eyes, shoving my worn boots in the sack. "What does it look like I'm doing?"

Emery studied me. "Leaving."

"Congratulations, you're correct."

A big frown now. "*Why* are you leaving?"

I faced him, hand on my hip. "Because I'm going home for the night."

"But isn't this your home now?"

I had both hands on my hips now. "Why would it be?"

Oh, he chose his words *carefully.* "Because you're my wife?"

I gave him a blank, cold stare, brows raised.

Emerys shifted uncomfortably. "And it's . . . you know. They prepared the eastern tower for us."

What a naïve little thump. I smiled, letting a small laugh escape. "And you thought I'd *willingly* dive into bed with you?"

I didn't think his cheeks could become any redder, but somehow, they did. "It-it's expected for us to consummate the marriage."

I threw my makeshift bag over my shoulder and turned for the entrance. All I wanted was my straw mat, to curl up under my ragged blanket with my cat and pretend this night had never happened. I shook my head. "What part of this is *expected* to you? Not knowing your bride's name until you exchange vows? Is that normal where you're from?"

"Actually, yes." He made to follow me. "Most of my brothers wed in similar situations."

"How terrible for you and your rich brothers." I crooned as I opened the door.

He stepped in front of me, dark hair falling in his eyes. *Why does he have to be so pretty?* "What about the peace?" Emerys asked. "Nothing can change without our union."

Are all men this desperate? Oh wait, of course, they are. I gestured toward the hall, the castle itself. "The state of our non-existent marriage bed won't affect the morale of your new people one lick. Trust me."

He opened his mouth to argue but was interrupted by a distant, stomach-turning horn call—the sound one I knew in my very bones.

Drystan's horn—a warning.

I lunged for the door, dropping my bag as my heart lodged in my throat. *Not again, not again. Please, not again.* I nearly fell on my backside as a firm grip yanked my elbow. Emerys' eyes were wide. "What was *that?*"

I jerked away from him. "Wildmen."

Those lovely eyes fixed onto me, filled with genuine fear. "I thought they were a myth. A scary story to keep wandering travelers out of Gwent."

Straightening, I said. "They're not a myth—they're savages. They steal and pillage, and if you ever touch me like that again, I'll pull your tongue out through your nostrils."

To my surprise, Emerys smiled. "That's demented."

"Get used to it," I hissed. "Now, let me pass. My brother needs me."

"You'd make demands of your prince?"

"Get. Out. Of. My. Way." I could have clawed off his smooth skin. "Or I will—"

"Torture me in some way, I'm sure." Emerys' smiled waned. "How do you think *you'll* stop the Wildmen?"

"Watch me and find out." I slid past him, and before I broke into a full sprint, I turned and spat. "And if you want to be useful, alert the others. Lord forbid I have to do everything myself."

6

"An unfortunate end to an unfortunate night."

Surprised shouts and whispers followed me from the castle. Maybe in the keep they'd also heard Drystan's warning —or perhaps they just wondered why their new princess sprinted through the halls like a wild animal.

I hit the castle doors at full speed. What was Drystan doing in the village while everyone else still celebrated? *Attending to his nightly chores, no doubt.* Unlike me, he'd always been so disciplined.

A rush of cold air kissed my cheeks, snaking around my ankles as I finally made it outside. On foot, I ran the muddy lane leading to the village, just a sparkling mirage on a dark horizon. My lungs burned as badly as my thighs, and I cried out as a sharp rock pierced my foot. I'd long lost my slippers. I slipped, icy mud squishing through my toes, but I didn't slow.

Shrill voices called out to each other as I grew closer—other villagers who must have left the feast early. Gasping, I scooped a large rock from the ground. It wasn't a knife, but at least I wouldn't be defenseless.

As I reached the edge of the village, I willed my breathing to slow along with my steps. My foot stung, but I ignored it. Illuminated by the few remaining torches, every door in Town Hall lay open. Tables were thrown into the street, along with the leftover supplies from the wedding preparations—but no immediate signs of danger.

Even so, I kept my body low, steps light. *They're scavenging. I have to find Drystan before he does something stupid.*

I kept away from the torchlight as I crept through the side streets, slowly making my way toward home. I'd never seen the village so empty. Behind me, overlooking from atop the hill, the castle shone like a star in the night. Was anyone coming to help? I couldn't have been the only one to hear Drystan's call. God help him if Emerys didn't sound the alarm—that useless, lovely, piece of man meat.

I gripped my makeshift weapon tighter as I moved into the west district. My foot bled, leaving a bread crumb trail of my path through the village. I turned the corner to the blacksmith's shop and sucked in a sharp breath—they'd turned it upside down. Bits of metal scraps and ore lay strewn across the shop yard. Steam seeped out into the cold night air, a quenched forge.

My pulse raced. Where's Caddic? I thought back. I'd seen him in the crowd at the ceremony, drinking and flirting with the girl from Emerys' carriage. Hopefully he'd remained at the ceremony. He'd lose his already loose top when he saw the state of his home.

Creeping toward the entrance, I grit my teeth, nails scraping against the stone in my hand, ready to bludgeon anyone in my way.

"*Rhia?*"

My blood turned to ice. I wheeled. "Drystan?"

"Here." A faint voice called. I rushed inside, and he sat

sprawled on the shop floor, perched on one arm. He smiled. "How do I look?"

"Lord Almighty." I dropped to my knees beside him and inspected the gash streaming blood over his eye. I tore off my dress sleeve—it was ruined anyway—and pressed it to the wound. "Hold that."

He replaced his hand with mine.

I glanced around—the shop had been stripped clean. I exhaled a shaky breath. "Wildmen?"

Drystan nodded, wincing. "Yeah."

"Are you hurt anywhere else?"

He tried to rise but fell back, gripping his side. "Just some bruised ribs, I think. They stole all the tools they could carry. Seems they heard about the wedding."

I rocked back onto my heels and sighed. "This is my fault."

"Shove off." Drystan hissed as he got to his feet. "It wasn't your choice to marry that pampered collie."

I wrapped his arm around my neck, mine around his waist. I'd allow myself to wallow later. "Let's get you home."

"I got blood on your dress."

"I don't care about my dress."

"Mama worked so hard on it."

I bit down on the inside of my cheek. "Did you see how many there were?"

Drystan hung against me, making my shoulders ache. "Four or five. Just a small raid. I caught them red-handed, and one hit me with a shovel before they took off."

I grimaced. "And here I thought you were unstoppable."

He let out a pained laugh, and something struck me. "What were you doing down here, anyway?"

After a momentary pause, Drystan's face drained of color as he opened his mouth to answer. "No—Sir Shellsworth."

He took off at a limp, basically dragging me under his arm.

As we hobbled toward our hut, angry cries floated down the hill from the castle—the others must have finally caught on.

Mama and Papa's property lay on the outer edge of the village, closer to the forest. As our hut came into view, Drystan jerked away from me, letting out a small sob. I let him go, freezing in my tracks.

They'd ransacked our home, too. The window shutters hung in half, the door smashed in.

Jacc.

I sprinted toward the door, Drystan crouched beside it. *If those dung-holes hurt my cat—*I screamed, "*Jacc!*"

A soft mewing came from the kitchen, under the flipped table. I chucked it aside, nearly weeping in relief at the sight of the orange lump, lying curled up in a ball. He looked up at me with squinted yellow eyes and rumpled coat. He'd probably slept through the whole thing. I scooped him up into my arms, pressing my face into his fur. Jacc just purred.

Drystan hobbled through the door, tears in his eyes. "They took him."

My heart sank. "Sir Shellsworth?"

Drystan nodded, voice cracked. "They kidnapped them all."

I followed him outside, and sure enough, they'd destroyed his snail farm. Drystan was probably the only person in the village that loved snails, kept them as pets. He fed them, talked to them, loved them like I loved Jacc. As much as I hated the creatures, I cried for him, resting my head on his shoulder. "I'm sorry."

Drystan shook his head, turning away, and limped to our bedroom. Even our straw mattresses were gone. He pursed his lips, cheeks flushed with anger. "They must have thought we were hiding gold away now that you're a princess."

I glared. "Don't call me that."

He shot me an equally sharp look, eyes filled with mourning.

"I'll stay here and clean up. You should go tell your *husband* what happened."

We starred at each other, tension cracking around us like lightning. *He blames me. Even though he said it wasn't my fault. He lied.*

I couldn't take it anymore. Turning, I stormed out, Jacc clinging to my shoulder.

———

"Where is he?" Mama grabbed my shoulders, eyes wild. I hadn't yet made it back into the village before she'd practically dove into me like a falcon on an oblivious rabbit. "Drystan?"

"He's at home." I shrugged out of her death grip, Jacc still in my arms. "He's fine. Just a few bangs and bruises."

"Praise God." Mama exhaled and kissed my forehead before jogging past me, heading toward our hut. I straightened my dress, scowling. *Love you, too, Mama.* No questions if *I* was okay, even with the blood drying on my sleeves.

A familiar yet hurried *click-click* met my ears, and I turned. Sweat poured down Papa's bright red face as he rushed toward me as quickly as his peg leg would allow. When he saw me, he slowed, sagging in relief. "Rhi-Rhi."

I allowed myself to fall into his arms, pressing my face against his shoulder as he held me close. I closed my eyes, absorbing the meat-heavy scent of his skin. *When was the last time Papa hugged me?* Jacc hissed, squished against my father's chest.

Kissing my hair, Papa whispered. "Are you hurt?"

"No," I lied, pulling away, struggling to keep ahold of the cat. "Drystan's a bit worse for wear, but—" My eyes began to well. "They took everything—again. How are we going to survive? We needed that ore to—"

"Hush, hush." Papa cupped my cheek. "That's a worry for

tomorrow. For tonight, go to the caste. Get some sleep." He nodded, grunting. "Tomorrow, we'll start over. That's all we can do."

Papa hobbled past me, the *click-click* of his leg growing more distant with every step. I turned, heading deeper into the village. The throbbing in my feet nearly unbearable. I sucked in every tear threatening to escape my eyes, refusing to let them show. I wasn't two steps past Town Hall when Emerys' figure appeared out of the gloom.

I bristled at the sight of him. *Great.* I wasn't in the mood to talk to anyone, let alone to his royal highness.

The prince's eyes widened as he took in the blood and mud coating me from head to toe, at the oversized cat clawing to escape my grip. I must have looked vicious because Emerys raised his hands as I approached. "Are you alright—"

"You want cooperation?" I hissed, pointing toward the Wentwood. "Stop them. We have so little, and they take *every-thing* we have. We have *nothing* now. Send your armies and take back what's ours."

Emerys stiffened, nostrils flaring. "What armies? Courtiers, maids, and known outcasts—that's what my father sent me to rule with. Are you suggesting they stab these Wildmen with knitting needles?"

I held his stare, choosing my words to wound. "What good is a prince without an army? What good are you, at all?"

Emerys took a step back, a pained expression flashing across his features before they set back into that trained boredom. His gaze dropped to Jacc, voice clipped. "What *is* that?"

I hugged Jacc tightly against my chest. "My cat."

"Why are you carrying it?"

"The Wildmen destroyed my home. Should I have left him in the ruins?"

Emerys gazed past me toward what remained of Town Hall —his words cold and emotionless as he said. "We're better to spend our energy reinforcing what we have remaining than running after them blindly."

I copied his tone. "Reinforce with what? We have no tools, no weapons. Unless you mean to send your enchanting nanny after them."

Another wince—Emerys' pale eyes scanned over me, narrowing. "Your feet are a mess. Please, head back to the castle. Let the healer look at them. I'll have someone help your family move their belongings to the South tower."

I didn't have the energy to argue anymore. "Fine, but I'm not sharing a bed with you."

He sniffed. "Fine."

I pushed past him, our shoulders colliding, and headed up the path toward the castle. If it had been a few hours earlier, the royals could have killed me for touching their prince that way.

But now I'm one of them, like it or not, and sweet Prince Emerys hadn't heard the last of Rhiannon Caddell.

7

"A pretty girl's tale."

I jolted awake as a soft knock tickled my door.

It took a moment to remember where I was—to adjust to the feel of a soft mattress beneath me rather than the usual sensation of straw stabbing my skin.

I'd just started to drift back to sleep when the knock came again. This time I jumped out of bed, wincing at the pain in my shredded feet, and cracked open the door. Hazel eyes peered at me from the other side. I recognized them immediately. *The prince's pretty friend.*

Throat dry as a tanning rack, I rasped. "Can I help you?"

"H-hello, my name is Wynny Beyron, we haven't officially met." The eyes blinked, lashes incredibly long. When I didn't answer, she added. "I'm your new handmaiden."

Handmaiden? I opened the door—mostly out of curiosity— and found the pretty girl from the carriage staring at me. With delicate steps, she moved through the door as I stepped aside.

She curtsied, and as she dipped, her thick dark spiral curls spilled over her bare shoulders, skin as creamy as the prince's.

I cocked my head, pursing my lips, mind still foggy. "Am I supposed to curtsy back?"

The girl—Wynny—smiled at me with slightly crooked front teeth. "If it pleases you, princess. You can do whatever you want, really."

"I don't think it works like that." I found myself smiling as I curtsied back, holding out the edges of the nightgown.

Wynny sucked in her wide pink lips, holding back a laugh.

My brows furrowed. "What?"

"Um, well, see—" Wynny hesitated, then held out the corners of her fancy emerald dress. "Keep your back straighter." She repeated the dipping movement, and I copied her, my thighs burning as I straightened.

I gave her a strained smile. "Better?

A quick nod. "Better."

Now that my mind had cleared, the bitterness of the previous night began to return. I folded my arms over my chest. "That's enough of that. What are you doing here, Lady Beyron?"

Wynny seemed surprised by the question and gestured to me, to the suite. "As I said, I'm here to be your handmaid."

"I saw you leave the prince's carriage yesterday."

More smiles. Wynny must like to smile. "Of course. I'm Prince Emerys' cousin."

That explains a lot. "And he's making you serve his bride?"

Wynny shrugged, casual. "I volunteered. In truth, we're second cousins." She waved flippantly. "I know—shocker. Lineage can be so confusing. But it was either this or marry Sir Cadogen."

I smirked. "What's wrong with Sir Cadogen?"

Wynny wrinkled her nose. "His beard is . . . icky. Plus, he's a butcher as well as a knight. His hands always stink. Also, I don't like eating animals. Yuck. I weighed my options, and this seemed better."

"Interesting." I rocked from hip to hip. "You don't eat meat?"

Another face. "Not unless I have to."

"Hmm." I folded my hands behind me. Wynny just watched me, expectant. "So, what do handmaids do?" I asked.

"Oh!" Wynny chirped, springing into action. She dashed into the bathing room, calling. "You must be wanting a bath, I presume? Your hair brushed? Nails trimmed? Brows plucked?"

Who plucks their eyebrows? I called back. "I bathed yesterday."

She peeked her head back into the room. "You don't bathe every day?"

"You do?"

Wynny let out an anxious giggle. "Breakfast, then? Are you hungry?"

I grinned. *Why do I like her?* "You've never been a handmaid, have you?"

"No, princess."

"That's okay." I sat on the sofa. "I've never been a princess, either."

Wynny's returning grin sparkled. "I guess we'll learn together." She dropped her chin. "I'll have the cooks make something for you."

My un-plucked brows rose. "We have cooks?"

"The prince hired a few from Aberaron."

"How indulgent of him."

Wynny's gaze flickered to the closet. "Your mother gave me your clothing sizes, and I had the seamstresses tailor them yesterday. I nearly overloaded the carriage with clothes before we left the city since I didn't know what you'd look like. Would you fair better in jewel or autumn tones? It was a mystery. Would you like help dressing?"

She talked to Mama? I tried not to let that bother me. *Plus, who needs help dressing?* Exhaling, I replied. "I can manage on my own, thank you."

Another curtsy. "I'll be back soon, then."

After Wynny left, the room felt empty without her. I leaned forward, rubbing my face in my hands, still exhausted from yesterday. What a wild turn my world had taken. From digging in the muck to having a closet full of gowns in one night.

My eyes rose to the closet, curiosity peaking. *She brought me clothes? Did they assume I had nothing respectable to wear?*

Despite my repulsion, I gently nudged open the closet door —and found it *filled* with gowns—dozens and dozens of them. Reds, golds, pinks, blues, purples, silver—each probably cost enough to repair every home in Lians.

And before you say, *"Rhia, why don't you just sell the dresses to pay Lians' debts?"* Let me tell you, that requires having someone to *sell* them to. The nearest town that could afford even *one* was over one hundred miles away.

If it weren't for the fact that all of my regular clothes were in the hut, I would have never considered wearing one. I glanced at the rumpled, stained pile of clothing on the floor by my bed. I could just wear my ruined wedding dress, if only to mortify the prince, but Mama and Papa didn't deserve that.

I sighed. *It's terrible to have a conscience.* Sifting through the selection, I found a simple bark-colored gown near the back of the closet. Its neckline was modest, the train meant to trail behind, but it was just the right length for me. I slipped it over my head and instantly became stuck. I struggled, jerking my arms wildly but to no avail.

No wonder Wynny asked if I wanted help. This is ridiculous. After a ten-minutes of struggling—peppered with more than a few curses—I finally got the bodice down over my shoulders. It took another twenty minutes just to lace it.

I looked in the mirror, and a slow smile crept across my face.

The rich brown looked pleasant against my golden waves and tanned skin. *Dare I say, I look pretty.*

"Did you forget the corset?" Wynny stood in the doorway, carrying a large tray of food.

I glanced down at myself and exhaled. "Was I supposed to wear one?'

Wynny let out a small, nervous chitter. "I'm sure no one will notice." She set the tray down on the low table in front of the sofa and lifted the lid—revealing an enormous helping of bacon, pork sausage, and duck eggs. Along with fresh tomatoes, laverbread, and toast. I just stared at it in shock. *They must have brought food from the capital city, too. This didn't come from Lians.*

Wynny placed a pot of tea beside the tray, then slowly turned to leave, letting out a long sigh. "Enjoy. I don't know how you'll ever manage to eat *all* of that by yourself. It's a feast for two, really."

I raised my hand. "Wait—"

She glanced over her shoulder, back arched, fluttering her lashes. "Yes, princess?"

This is so silly. I chewed my lip. "Would you like to have breakfast with me? I'll eat the meat."

Wynny let out an excited squeal then clapped. "I hoped you'd ask. It all smells so good." She paused, hand over her mouth, eyes widening. "But . . . princesses aren't supposed to eat with their staff."

I let out a quick laugh. "Well, seeing that I've been a princess for less than twenty-four hours, I still haven't received the rule book. Come sit with me."

Another squeal, and Wynny plopped down on the sofa, patting the space beside her. I sat, just then noticing she already had two teacups on the tray. I couldn't hold back my smile.

As if reading my thoughts, Wynny poured a cup for each of us. Inhaling the steam, it smelled like dandelion. Bitter yet pleasant. I took a sip and sighed, sinking into the sofa's soft cushions. *Lord in Heaven, this tastes wonderful.*

Wynny stuck her fork into one of the fat tomatoes, cutting it into quarters. Humming, she bobbed her head as if listening to a tune that only she could hear. She seemed so positive, bright. I'd never had a female friend before, maybe—

I shook my head. *Another ruse, stay focused, Rhia.* "Tell me about your life in Aberaron. What was it like?" I sipped my tea.

"There's not much to tell," Wynny said through a mouth full of tomato. "My father is the King's cousin. He owns some land on the edge of the region. My mother and I sit inside all day and knit, or stitch, and on exciting days, we garden."

"Exhilarating," I said, hoping to keep the conversation flowing.

Nodding, she swallowed then took a bite of toast. Stomach growling, I bit into a slice of bacon and nearly groaned—so wonderfully salty.

"We only traveled to the palace on special occasions." Wynny continued. "So, I only saw Emerys those few times, but we always got on well. Out of all the King's son, Emerys is the only one that made a point of making me feel welcome."

My stomach clenched. I didn't want to hear about Emerys' goodness, especially after how I'd treated him last night.

"Then—" Wynny paused dramatically, eyes glittering. "Father betrothed me to Sir Cadogen."

I gasped, hand over my mouth. "How terrible!"

"Oh, it was." Wynny drawled, not catching my mocking tone. "I knew my life would surely be over after that, but then I heard the prince was being sent away to be wed. After many secret letters to the palace, I finally received one back—Emerys' invitation for me to join him in Gwent." She smiled. "I accepted in a heartbeat. My father was so angry he cut off my betrothal to Sir Cadogen." Another smile. "Tragic."

Chuckling, I shoved the rest of the bacon strip into my

mouth, thinking as I chewed. "Did Emerys bring others? Besides the cooks, servants, and yourself?" *Did he lie about the soldiers just to avoid a fight? Please, tell me he lied.*

She shook her head. "No, Emerys is quiet, but from what I heard, the King didn't let him bring anyone else but Catrin." On the last word, I didn't miss the way Wynny's eyes flicked to me then back to her plate.

Oh yes, I hadn't forgotten about Catrin. Had the older woman been talking about me already?

I licked bacon grease off my lips, taking another sip of tea. "Tell me about Catrin."

Wynny paused mid-chew. "I—I don't know much of her life before the palace, but with six sons, it's easy to understand why the queen would hire some extra help." She leaned in closer, whispering. "I don't know if you've heard, but most royals don't care for their own babies."

I gaped, taken aback. "The prince wasn't raised by his mother?"

Wynny returned to eating. "It's not uncommon."

I sunk into the cushion, shame settling on my bones. "How horrible."

I couldn't imagine my life without Mama and Papa now, even at sixteen, but all through childhood? All the times Mama sang me to sleep, stroking my hair. Papa carrying me on his shoulders before he'd lost his leg. I shook my head—I didn't want to think about that a moment longer than I had to.

"It's just another way of life," Wynny said, voice soft. "Anyway, Catrin is nice enough. Even though she's overprotective . . . and a bit stuffy." She scowled. "And she told me to cover up once, said I looked like a tart."

My eyes fell to Wynny's neckline for the first time—to her full breasts teetering on the edge of spilling free of her gown. Self-conscious, I glanced down at my own. While they weren't small, they weren't comparable to my handmaid's, nor did they stand at attention the way hers did. *No wonder she mentioned the corset.*

Flushed, I snagged a sausage off the tray. "And the prince? What's he like?"

Wynny sat down her fork, patting her mouth with a napkin, thoughtful. "He is, like I said, quiet, but I think that's what happens when your brothers always overtalk you. I remember once when my family came for a feast, his eldest brother spilled soup all over my gown. Instead of laughing with the others, Emerys helped me clean up before my parents found out and got mad about me making a spectacle of myself."

I cringed deeper into the sofa, panged with more guilt. "That was kind."

"It was." Wynny brushed crumbs from her cleavage and stood. "Speaking of Emerys, I almost forgot. He asked me to request that you attend to him when you're ready."

My brows rose. "*Attend* to him?"

Wynny giggled, cheeks reddening. "As in *speak* to him. I'm not foul."

I let my lips quirk into a grin. "You can be with me. I'll laugh."

She grinned back. "Glad to know. I'll return this evening but call if you need anything in the meantime."

"I will." Standing, I gave her my best attempt at a curtsy. "And when you return, bring two trays of food. I'd like to spend more time gossiping with Wynny Beyron, second cousin of the King's umpteenth son, who was betrothed to Sir Cadogen but decided to run away and become a maid, all while being scolded for her presumptuous breasts."

Wynny let out one of her high-pitched squeals before skipping out the door.

I took my time finishing breakfast, savoring every bite, but even that could only go on for so long. After running a brush through my hair for the three-hundredth stroke, I couldn't avoid it any longer.

I needed to attend to my husband.

Setting the brush back on the vanity, I smiled at my reflection before standing to remove my new gown.

He never specified that I had to be ready today.

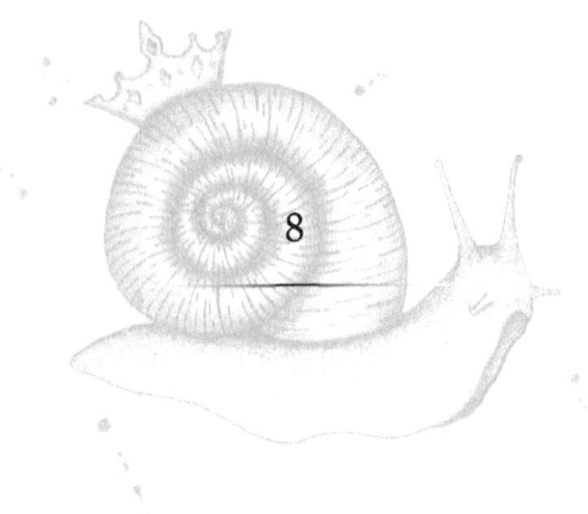

8

I wasn't ready the next day, either . . . or the next. Not for almost a week, despite Wynny's gentle, yet prodding, reminders.

Instead, I helped Mama and Papa repair their hut, ignoring their not-so-subtle remarks about my behavior. I ignored Drystan's comments about sucking it up, and getting the ordeal over with, as well. It wasn't their life, their body.

So, I just continued to ignore them.

Until I couldn't.

You could only pretend your problems didn't exist for so long—and by problems, I meant husbands. The dread, the anxiety—there were only so many ways to drown them with ignorance before they eventually found a way to break through.

Today was that day.

On the west side of the village, mist clung heavily to my cloak as I made my way across town, heading to the carpenter.

We'd raked together enough scrap wood to repair most of the damage to my parent's hut, but there were only so many times you could nail through a split grain and expect it to stay together.

Mama and Papa had returned to the hut, even in its disrepair, the night after the raid. *Too humid* is what Papa had said about his night in the castle. I think consumed by guilt would be more accurate for his emotions, especially after he'd seen the state of my feet. He'd accepted the King's offer, brought the prince to Lians. This was his fault. At least, that's what I kept reminding myself—anything to drown out the whispers of the obedient daughter struggling to remain in the depths of my heart.

With everyone trying to replace what they'd lost in the raid, the streets were bustling with shoppers clutching their meager wallets. I kept my eyes to the ground, limping slightly as my boots rubbed against the sore spots on my heels. I'd bundled up in Drystan's hat and scarf, hoping the crowd wouldn't recognize me. I just needed a new beam for the doorframe. If I could get through this without someone sneering "princess" at me, it would be a miracle.

Remember before when I said how much I hated crying?

You can imagine my displeasure as I tell you it's all my eyes seemed capable of doing now. Repulsive, I know. At night, alone in my room, the tears crept down my cheeks, dampening my pillow. Wynny often stayed with me late into the night, warding off the loneliness, but even she had to sleep at some point. The salty traitors threatened to unleash their unwanted tide with every mocking look and remark my people—*my people*—shot in my direction.

My pity party was interrupted as a hooded figure knocked into my arm—hard. "Watch it," I hissed as the figure bounced off my muscled bicep, nearly hitting the ground in a comical spiral.

A lock of dark hair escaped his hood as a familiar voice whispered, "My apologies."

I froze. The figure hurried off in the direction I'd come, turning the corner out of the west district and toward my family's property.

Emerys? Of all the days. Couldn't he let me wallow in peace? My feet turned to follow him before my mind had willed it, my eyes narrowing. *What's he up to?* If he'd wanted to be sneaky, he shouldn't have worn perfectly polished leather boots with brass buckles—idiot.

A worn narrow lane led from the main part of Lians toward my hut, and if you continued on, to the Wentwood forest. As he followed the path, Emerys paused every few meters to glance over his shoulder, the storm clouds matching the turmoil in his eyes.

He thinks he's being followed. How arrogant. Almost like he thinks he's a prince or something. I smiled to myself, tucking behind a nearby tree. As he continued, I pulled away from my hiding place, sap clinging to my fingers. Instead of heading toward the Wentwood, as I expected, he turned right at the fork in the lane, heading straight for my family's hut.

I watched, eyes narrowing. *What's he after?*

My cover was gone, but from where I stood atop the rise, I could see everything happening at the hut below. I dropped to my belly, content to watch as Emerys knocked on what remained of my parent's door, laughing internally as he shooed away the chickens gathering around his feet, pecking at his shiny buckles.

Drystan and Papa were out in the horse pens, shoveling muck, but Mama had been cooking when I'd left for the carpenters. Sure enough, she appeared in the doorway, shock coloring her expression when she realized who stood outside her home. She curtsied, plaid skirt immaculate, and Emerys bowed in response. After exchanging a few words I couldn't hear, Emerys' entire demeanor drooped. I watched as Mama invited him inside, concerned, but Emerys shook his head—a refusal.

Mama wrung her hands as he turned—heading back up the lane—and as I ducked out of the way, a thought struck me. *He's looking for me.*

Not that the notion should be odd. I am his wife after all, but that wasn't the reason he came to my home . . . why he looked so defeated.

It's because I was too much of a coward to make the first move, to break the silence between us. He is—unfortunately—a part of Lians now, and instead of welcoming him, I shut him out like a dog that'd rolled in a cow pie. Shaming the hospitality of my people.

I grit my teeth, cursing before I stood. I couldn't let him make a fool of me like this. I wouldn't be the one known as a coward. That was his job. There would only be one victor in this stand-off of ours, and it would be me. As you can imagine, I hauled my buttocks back to the castle, picturing all the ways I'd make him suffer for this slight, the carpenter wholly forgotten.

———

I dressed in the same brown gown I wore that first day—fully cinched in a corset this time. I turned, admiring myself in the mirror at every angle. Even if my top half had nothing on Wynny's, other parts of me had developed just fine, and this dress accentuated it perfectly. I grinned. *Checkmate, Emerys, your move.*

When I left my suite, I didn't expect to see so many . . . strangers. Did I just not notice them before, or I had my mind purposely blocked them out?

Wynny had mentioned a few servants, but I counted twenty just in the hall directly outside my room. Scrubbing the floors, the walls, the ceiling, putting fresh candles in the goat horn sconces. If I had to give Emerys one thing, it's that he didn't waste any time. This place would be tourist worthy within the month.

They watched me from the corners of their eyes as I passed. I smoothed my dress, pulling my hair over my chest, self-conscious. *I shouldn't have worn the corset.*

It must be mid-day now. I shouldn't have slept so late. As I passed the window, I glanced outside. The sky remained its usual grey hue, the horizon nearly black. Rain and possibly a thunderstorm would be arriving soon. I could smell it in the air.

I reached the grand entry outside the dining hall. Servants traveled up and down the polished wood staircases, all in some sort of a rush. In the week they'd been here, I hadn't once seen the prince's company leave the castle. Afraid of being spat on by locals, most likely.

A portly woman began her descent as I approached the stair-case. As she brushed by me on the steps, I cleared my throat. "Excuse me?"

She glanced over her shoulder, annoyed at the interruption, then her features instantly shifted to alarm when she realized who I was. Wheeling, she dipped into a rushed curtsy. "Princess, how may I serve?"

Bile rose in my throat. *Serve.* I didn't want to be served— I wanted them to *leave.* I inhaled. "Ma'am, do you know what room the prince has occupied?"

As the woman lifted her chin, confusion flickered in her eyes. "Isn't he—" She smiled a little. "East tower, princess. Shall I send for him?"

"No, but thanks for the help." My thighs couldn't handle another curtsy, so I bowed at the waist before moving past her on the stairs. Halfway up, sniggers echoed behind me, and I turned. Head-to-head with another servant, the portly woman whispered something before they both burst into giggles.

They know I'm not sharing the prince's bed. Fists clenched, I cleared my throat again, watching as their faces drained of color and they slowly looked up at me. *No wonder the prince does it all the time. It's not allergies. It's a good way to get attention.* I gave them a dangerous smile. "Ladies, is something *funny*? May I join in on the joke?"

Each of them spewed out a stream of lame excuses before sprinting from the entry.

I smirked to myself, rather proud of my small victory. Dumb ninnies.

———

Too many bloody stairs.

Of course, the prince would pick the room at the top of the tallest tower. *Should I expect a dragon guarding him? Or worse . . . an ogre and his pet?* The staircase spiraled, up, up, up—the end nowhere in sight. Every step threatened to end me. I could walk for miles without a labored breath, but at an incline? *I'd rather be dead.*

When I finally reached the top, I leaned against the wall, trying to catch my breath. *I haven't even spoken to him yet, and I'm ready to leave.* Wheezing, I wiped the sweat dripping down my face on my sleeve. *I can't go in looking like this.* Smoothing my hair, I pulled it over my shoulder so it fell in one long wave to my hip, strands clinging to my damp palms.

Inhaling, I reached to knock on the prince's door, then hesitated. Should I knock softly? That would be lady-like . . . but a firm, loud knock would project more confidence. Two big knocks? One *giant* knock? Maybe—

"Are you just going to stand in the way like an old, blind dog?"

I nearly screamed, stomach leaping into my ribs, and turned. Catrin stood behind me, sneering, wearing a casual green scarf today, a stack of papers sat in her bony arms. When I didn't answer, she waved me off. "If you plan on remaining a pothole, at least do it in the corner. Some of us have work to do, and I don't have the time or energy to climb over your obtrusive backside."

Definitely an ogre. I cocked my head, smiling sweetly. "You're right—I do have a lot of work to do, thank you for noticing. I'm surprised you're awake. Don't vampire bats only come out after dark?"

Catrin scoffed, pushing past me. "As do harlets, I've heard, but here you are." She walked straight into the prince's room— no knock.

I should have thought of that. Scowling, I followed Catrin into the suite.

Emerys sat at a large desk in the back corner of the chamber. With the fire stoked, the air inside was sweltering. His suite looked nearly identical to mine in size and decoration, I noted smugly. Several gigantic bags lay on the ground beside his pristinely made bed—personal belongings. A folded cloak sat on the end.

I smirked. *Catrin probably straightens his blankets for him.*

Emerys remained intensely focused on the book in his hands, accepting the papers Catrin handed him without acknowledging her.

Catrin smiled at me—at least, I think it was a smile—her teeth stained yellow. "Found this one sitting outside like an open-mouthed guppy. Didn't know your loud-mouthed wife was also busy body, did you?"

Emerys jerked straight, eyes wide, hair still slightly damp from his walk.

My face grew hot and *not* from the blazing hearth. I crossed my arms over my chest. "I was *not* spying if that's what you're implying."

"Really?" Catrin shot back. "Then what were you doing, you dim-witted—"

Emerys stood. *"Catrin!"*

I raised a finger, lips pursed, and to my surprise, Emerys quieted. I turned to elderly woman, jerking my chin toward the closed-up window. "I'm curious, what do you think your bones would sound like hitting the ground from this height?"

Poor Emerys. I'd never seen someone look so terrified, eyes darting between us frantically.

After a profoundly wrinkled scowl, Catrin chuckled and began a slow hobble toward the door. As she passed me, she whispered, "Guppy."

"Hag," I shot back.

"Please, stop," Emerys whispered.

I held back a smile as the door closed behind me. Emerys sucked in a deep breath, running a hand over his pale face. "I apologize for that."

I shrugged one shoulder.

Emerys attempted a smile. "I'm glad you came. You've met Wynny, I take it?"

I smiled back, genuine. "She's a doll. The best part of our marriage."

"Indeed." Emerys' shoulders relaxed slightly, then he hesitated, nodding toward the door. "May I ask, what *were* you doing out there?"

"Um." I twisted my hair, cringing. "Trying to decide the best way to knock."

Emerys smiled again, returning to the seat behind his desk. I noticed the thick fur coat tightly wrapped around him.

"Cold?" I asked.

He nodded. "It's warmer closer to the coast." His eyes lifted and trailed along my simple gown. Part of me wanted to hate the approving gleam I saw there, but instead, I found myself relishing in it. I swished my hips. "Something wrong?"

Emerys blinked, cheeks reddening. "I was just—ah—I'm surprised you're not wearing a cloak."

My shoulders slumped. *Fine, then.* "I'm used to it . . . the cold."

"Would you like one?"

"A cold?"

"No." Emerys shifted. "A cloak."

"Oh." *Stupid.* I shook my head. "I have one already, thank you." Not that I'd mention that the moths had eaten holes in it, and the hem tore from snagging rocks on the road. I straightened. *No more beating around the bush.* "You sent for me?"

"Yes." Emerys' face brightened. Thankfully, he didn't mention the summons was from a week ago. Reaching under his desk, he pulled out a small bundle of potted, robust yellow flowers. He held them out to me, beaming. "For you."

I just stared at the flowers in his hand, blinking dumbly, stomach clenched. *I didn't prepare for this.* I looked up but didn't take them. "What are they?"

Still smiling. "Roses."

"We don't have roses in Gwent."

"I read as much. I brought them from Aberaron."

"Why?"

Now his expression began to sink. "For you."

An awkward silence passed, and not knowing what else to do, I took the roses and set them on the low table behind me. I brushed my fingertips along the petals. *So soft.* "I'd rather talk about what you plan to do about the raid."

Emerys let out a heavy sigh, sitting back in his chair and gesturing to the papers strewn over his desk. "This."

A pause. My brow rose, hand on my hip. "And what's *this*?"

"I had your father bring me the records of Lians' coffers, expenses, and financial dealings from the last five years." Emerys passed me a fresh piece of parchment. "Here's my totals."

I scanned over the note, taking in his calculations. "The coffers are empty. What did you expect?"

Emerys' lips spread into a coy smile. "You can read?"

I frowned, tossing back the paper. "Why did you hand this to me if you thought I couldn't?"

"I—" Those full lips stretched further into a grin. "A test, I guess."

I watched a bit of mischief pass over his features—and I hated that I didn't hate it. A thrill ran through me, and I leaned onto his desk. "Just ask me outright next time, will you? I'm just an ignorant peasant. Your court-trained tricks will just fly straight over my empty head."

Most men cowed or got angry when I pushed them, but Emerys surprised me when he leaned in closer, our faces a foot apart. "But they didn't, did they? You saw straight through me."

I jerked away, breaths shallow, and opened the window to let in some cool air. The rain had indeed begun to fall over the village, as I predicted. Behind me, Emerys' chair scraped against the stone floors as he stood. He joined me by the window, gazing down at Lians below. "Your father kept accurate records."

I snorted. "Papa has never kept records in his life."

He kept quiet as if expecting me to continue. I refused to acknowledge him.

"Then," Emerys whispered, "your brother?"

"I did." I watched a sparrow soar past the window, heading toward the village.

From the corner of my eye, I noticed the way Emerys seemed to fixate on it. "For all these years?" Surprise coated his tone.

"Yes." Finally, I turned, crossing my arms again as I leaned against the windowsill. "Someone had to do it. Is that a problem?"

Papa never saw the point in paper pushing, as he called it. Mostly, I'd started keeping the numbers just as something to do since the other girls never liked playing with me. It kept me busy, made me feel important.

Emerys shoved his hands in his coat pockets, the tip of his nose pink from the freezing air pouring in. "Of course not. At least, not for me." He paused, still focused on the sparrow, who'd landed in a bilberry bush. "But you, of all people, must realize there's no avoiding the King's tax. My father's patience with Lians is at an end. The deadline is coming due."

I wrapped my arms around myself. *How could Papa leave this on my shoulders? I thought we had more time.* How could he think that I could change Lians' fate—let alone the King's mind? Like a frightened animal backed into a corner, I bristled, gesturing to his desk. "You've seen for yourself. We have nothing . . . and after our wedding night, even less. Where, my dear husband, do you propose this gold is to come from?"

Emerys' eyes danced over the country spreading out in front of him, deep in thought. Did he realize it's his responsibility now? Every twig, fawn, blade of grass—all his.

Or, I should say, ours.

His eyes tightened. "There are always ways to cut back, increase trade. Gwent is a large region—"

"And you know nothing about it, do you?" I cut in. "Nothing about the people you supposedly mean to rule?"

Emerys shot me a look, one I couldn't read. "People. Land. In numbers, they're all the same."

Lians is not *the same. I am* not *the same.* An idea—a foolish one—struck me.

Exhaling, I slammed the window shut. I grabbed the cloak folded on his bed and tossed it to him. "You'll need this."

He caught it, brow arched. "Why?"

Because I need you to understand, I need you to convince your father to leave us alone before I let everyone down. I dug through the closet and found a beat-up cloak left behind in an old dresser. I slipped it on. "We're going for a walk."

He looked surprised, but I saw through his act. "In this weather?"

I sneered and repeated. "Is that a problem?"

Emerys gave me a knowing, crooked grin but didn't answer. I couldn't hide my smug smile as I heard his footsteps follow me out the door.

"Recreational thinking."

T he rain shifted into a full-blown deluge as Emerys and I walked the mile down to the village. He didn't complain as I'd expected. More than once, he slipped in the mud, having to catch himself against the cold, wet ground. But every time he did—with a straight face—he got right back up, wiping his hands clean on the inside of his cloak.

I traveled the road with ease, just happy to be free from the castle again. It wasn't so bad, honestly. I enjoyed having my own room. I enjoyed the privacy and being able just to shut my door, knowing that I could block out the world and everyone in it. No one bothered me except for Wynny, but I didn't mind her. In fact, I looked forward to our meals together, to our chats and banter.

I'd only gone to the dining hall once since the ceremony. The prince had been there, eating with the rest of his staff. He'd tried to catch my eye. Instead of the seat beside him, I sat with Wynny, choosing to ignore him completely.

Papa hadn't been happy when he'd found out. *The future of Lians depends on you, and you've chosen now to act like a spoiled brat. I thought I taught you better.*

Wincing, I shook my head to chase away the memory.

Out of the corner of my eye, I caught Emerys watching my feet, expression intense.

But I can't ignore him today, can I? Finally, I asked. "What are you staring at?"

He blinked up at me, rain dripping over his dark lashes. "You're so surefooted. How?"

I smiled. "Lots of practice."

Emerys just nodded, focus deepening on my filthy boots.

As we made it to the edge of the village, I pointed out the dilapidated fencing surrounding its borders. "Because we're in the lowlands, the village floods this time of year." I ran my hand along the worn, warped railing and kicked the post supporting it. It slid to the left about three inches. I leaned against it, listening to it *slurp* in the muck. "The water settles in deep. Without stone, our foundations don't hold."

Emerys' eyes narrowed, but he stayed quiet as he followed me deeper into Lians. He did better keeping upright on the main streets—which were dirt in the summer and sludge during the rainy season.

Eyes watched us from their homes as we passed through the Eastside. Some lucky villagers still had glass in their windows— most had broken out during the years of Wildmen raids. The thatched rooves of several of the homes had rotted. The fenced-in yards directly outside their front doors held together with twine, leaving enough gaps in the fence for their dogs to slip free and roam during the night.

The eyes that watched followed us as we continued deeper, toward the heart of the village. Were my people more surprised to see the prince and me together, or that a host of guards didn't surround him? *If only he'd brought guards. Then, at least, he'd be useful.*

I glanced over my shoulder, shuddering as rain dripped down my neck. Emerys' gaze bounced from house to house—taking in every detail, every cracked stone and lichen-stained rock.

This one's a thinker. I wasn't sure what to make of it—of him.

We reached Town Hall. The front entry sat open, and a woman stood in the doorway sweeping the stone floors—the last of the destruction—and added it to the mud outside. Furniture leaned against the hitching posts, in various states of repair. Smoke rose from the chimney, blending into the gray sky above.

"There's no smoke coming from the huts." I turned toward his soft voice. Emerys nodded toward the villager's homes, brows pinched. "Why is that?"

"Dry wood is scarce," I answered, bundling myself deeper into my cloak. "It's more effective to heat one building and let the people sleep inside on nights too cold for just a blanket."

"Don't you cut and dry firewood during the summer?" he asked.

I bristled. He spoke like it was such an obvious solution. "Lians has a small population, and most of the men are old. Only so many trees can be felled, cut, and stacked in the short dry months we have. We do the best we can."

Emerys' eyes shifted to Town Hall, taking it in. "Wood can be bought, as can stone."

"I already told you, we don't have the money."

"There's always trade," he added. "What do you have that Lians can barter with?"

I stepped closer, nearly snarling, holding his stare. He didn't back down. "What do *we* have, you mean? And nothing. Lians hasn't traded in decades since our last stone quarry stopped supporting us. We can barely feed the little livestock we have.

What grains we produce, we grind for our food. There's nothing."

Emerys shook his head, defiant. "There has to be something."

Lord, how do I make him get it? On impulse, I stepped forward and looped my arm through his, crooning. "Follow me."

He did.

And as we walked in silence through the streets, his eyes continued to absorb every detail they could find—the stray cats hunting the rats ducking in and out of the grain rooms. The children slipping outside to play in the rain, only to be brought in by their mothers' angered shouts. Drystan and I had been just like them once, playing whether it rained or shined.

I missed those days—when we didn't have any cares. When we snuck out into the fields to pick dandelions, smashing them onto our faces to turn our cheeks yellow. Mama always hated that. She'd take her rags and scrub our skin raw. The next day, we'd just go out and do it again. I didn't know why she bothered.

Had the prince ever played like that? Not caring what the next day would bring, let alone the next hour? No, probably not, but still, I didn't feel sorry for him. At least . . . I tried not to.

The sharp crack of a hammer against anvil welcomed us to the blacksmith's—which looked more like a horse shed now-a-days than a hut. The pounding echoed from within the small, enclosed space, leaking out across the yard. Along with the forge, it was the only building in the village with an actual smokestack.

As we grew closer, the hammer beats stopped.

A large puddle had formed outside the entrance. Without pausing, Emerys hopped over it, holding out his hand for me so I could do the same. Smirking, I trudged through the mirky water, letting it soak into my boots and cloak. *Checkmate.*

Emerys rolled his eyes, letting out a breathy huff.

Hanging leather strips served as a front entrance, bound and tied to a rod across the top of the doorway. A bell tinkled as we entered.

The heat emitting off the forge was breathtakingly wonderful. Emerys shuffled towards it, rubbing his gloved hands together, his pale cheeks bright pink from the cold. Rows and rows of shelves lined the walls, empty spaces left behind in the dust where tools had once sat—probably stolen in the recent raid. From deeper inside the shop, a deep, gruff voice called. "Who's there?"

Emerys stiffened. I held back my grin as I called back. "Just me, Cad."

The prince's brows lifted, suspicious. "Cad?"

I couldn't hold it back anymore. My lips spread into a grin. "Jealous?"

A few moments later, Caddic stepped into the shop's central area, only an apron covering his shirtless torso, sweat dripping down over the leather. In his early twenties, enormous was an understatement when it came to Caddic. I think it's the reason he'd always been partial to me—I was the only girl in the village he couldn't physically snap over his knee.

Caddic ran a cloth over the rough blade in his thick, calloused hands. He smiled at me, pushing his curls away from his damp forehead. "Good to see you, Rhia—or am I supposed to call you princess now?"

I snorted. "Call me that, and I'll bust your teeth out. Where's Alys?"

"Napping in the back. The hammer beats always put her to sleep." Caddic's eyes made an amused pass over Emerys. "You're the prince?"

To his credit, Emerys kept his voice clear and steady, something I'd seen larger men falter within the presence of Caddic's rippling pectorals. "I am."

The blacksmith cocked his head. "How old are you?"

"Seventeen," Emerys answered.

"You're small."

Emerys smiled, court trained and venomous. "You're absurdly large."

Caddic let out a booming laugh. "Touche." A pause. "Do you expect me to bow?"

Emerys never let that toothy smile falter. If he felt intimidated, he didn't let it show. "Yes, but if the wrap around your midline is any clue, you have pain in your lower back. I wouldn't want to strain you."

Caddic frowned.

My eyes flashed to Emerys, widening. *A thinker and observant.* I'd never noticed Caddic's brace.

Smooth as silk, Emerys stepped toward the white-hot forge, inspecting it. "An exquisite piece. What was taken from you in the raid?"

Caddic set his blade down on the stool beside him. He dabbed his face with his cloth, leaning against his anvil. "Most of my hammers and tongs. All my good steel—which wasn't much to begin with." He cocked his head again. "Why? Do you have something shiny for me under those pajamas?"

Again, Emerys held his composure. "Make a list of your missing materials and have it sent to the castle." After that, he turned on his heel, splashing through the puddle as he left the shop.

I glanced at Caddic, who made a swirling gesture at his temple, nodding to Emerys. I rolled my eyes and followed after the prince. *That didn't go as I'd hoped.*

Outside, the rain had slowed to a misting. Out of earshot, Emerys stood with his eyes closed, sucking in deep breaths. For a moment—so brief—I thought I caught the welling of tears in his lashes. As I approached, he turned to me—they were gone. "I know what you're trying to do. I get it—the posturing isn't necessary."

I scowled. "Posturing?"

"Lians is in a terrible state. I see that," Emerys continued. "But I can't change the law. What's owed is owed."

Part of me wanted to fall apart. Another part of me wanted to tackle him to the ground and shake him until he took back the words. Trembling, I said. "We. Have. Nothing. To. Pay. With. No wood, no steel, barely any livestock. We can't even repair the damage we've already taken."

My voice rose too loudly. Caddic watched us from the edge of his shop, along with a few other damp figures peeking around the corners. From our vantage point, the mudflats were visible in the distance. I pointed. "The rains have ruined our fields. We have no crops to gather, no food to send to the palace, let alone feed ourselves." Breath shaking, I lowered my tone for only him to hear. "We'll starve. Both of us. Your daddy isn't here to feed you anymore."

I expected Emerys to lash out—as I would—but instead, he began to pace. Scanning the people watching, expression as stormy as the sky above. His gaze locked onto a middle-aged woman snooping from a thatch in her roof. "You, ma'am," Emerys called, and she shrank back until only her nose and eyes were visible.

She squeaked. "My lord?"

Emerys smiled brightly. "Do you have any sons, daughters?"

"One of each, my lord." More of her slim face became visible. "Both young, but strong."

"Do you have any shovels?"

"Three, I think."

"Send your children out with them," Emerys said gently. "Tell your neighbors to do the same."

The woman huffed but nodded, disappearing into her loft.

I stepped toward him. "What are you doing?

Emerys shot me a stiff smile. "If you want your crops to survive, you need to provide the proper drainage."

I rested my hand on my hip, still speaking loud enough for

the others to hear. "And you know how to provide that? Better than our farmers that have been toiling in this earth longer than we've been alive?"

"And like you said before, they're too old to work," Emerys countered. "Since I was useless to him, my father always made sure I had the most menial tasks possible." As he spoke, a boy and a girl—maybe ten and twelve years old—emerged from the woman's hut, carrying a stack of shovels. "And lo and behold." Emerys nodded to them as he continued. "I was placed in charge of recreational agriculture."

"Recreational?"

Emerys nodded. "Traditional farming is becoming a thing of the past. Mass grows with a set purchase price and transport. That's the future."

Buyable food you don't grow yourself? I swallowed, throat dry. Did Papa not know about this? Had he purposely kept this from me? *No, he'd had told me if he knew.* But in truth, I wasn't sure anymore.

I shook my head, chasing the thought away. "Agriculture. How very peasant of you."

Emerys smiled at me, truly smiled, and my insides did a strange fluttering. "Indeed. Would you like to see how a peasant works?"

———

Less than an hour later, we had six kids and ten shovels collected. The rain, thankfully, decided to hold off for now. I wondered if the weather watched us with as much curiosity as the villagers surrounding the flats, whispering to one another as I imagined the raindrops did. Hopefully, a few more volunteers would come, but I doubted it. Who wanted to work in shin-high mud, especially under the prince's orders?

And oh—the water had pooled deep. From atop the hill

overlooking the flats, the land looked like a lake. I listened as Emerys rattled off a list of instructions on how to dig proper drain trenches. About how we'd cut out an artificial pond at the end of the field to give the water to somewhere to pool. How we'd slope the trenches so the extra rain would run straight into the pond instead of drowning future crops.

Once the children—now enthusiastic and bright with excitement—had started, Emerys rejoined me at the top of the hill. He raised his hands. "Well?"

I shrugged and sighed. "I guess even without an army, you might be good for something."

Emerys beamed.

I picked up a shovel, leaning it over my shoulder. He gave me a questioning look and asked. "Where are you going?"

"Starting the day's work, of course." I batted my lashes at him, the way I'd seen Wynny do at the village boys. "What are *you* doing, darling?"

I loved every time my words shocked him. "But, you're soaking wet."

"So are they." I nodded toward the children, then leaned in close, placing my hand on his shoulder. "Better grab a shovel, too, princeling. Your subjects are watching."

Sure enough, half the village had arrived. Some young, but mostly the elderly, crotchety folks, irritated that the prince would dare make a change to their precious land without at least a six-week meeting to argue the matter.

I giggled as the confident smile slid from Emerys' lips, but—to his credit—he picked up a shovel, all the same. "I said I was placed in charge of agriculture. Not that I'd actually done the manual work."

I guessed as much. I just shrugged and continued down the hill towards the fields, hips swaying. Emerys followed.

When I looked back, Caddic bent to pick up a shovel, as well.

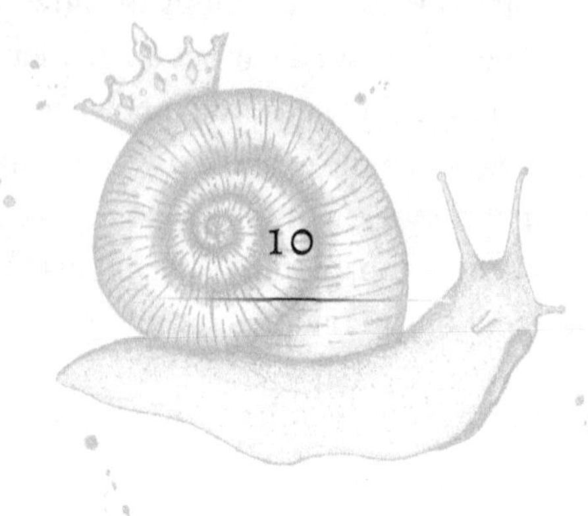

10

"Sparks in the mud."

"**F**ilthy, hateful beasts." Emerys flapped his dirt-stained hand like a panicked chicken's wings, sending a snail airborne. Yanking my shovel from the ground, I bit down on my lower lip to hold back the laughter bubbling in my throat.

"There's so many," Emerys cursed, wiping snail slime on his trouser leg. "How are there so many?"

"It's always been like this." I straightened, back aching from hours of digging. The sky had cleared as mid-day shifted toward evening. We probably had about two hours of daylight left. "They've been here long before Lians was founded and will be here long after."

"How? Why? I need answers." Emerys split another poor creature with the tip of his shovel. Good thing Drystan wasn't here. I hated to admit, but the prince looked rather attractive with that smear of mud across his cheek, dark hair rumpled

82

from the rain. I shook my head to chase away the thought, then shrugged. "It's a mystery."

"It must be the habitat," Emerys mused, primarily to himself, scanning the flats. All our original volunteers remained—even Caddic. Digging, digging, digging—endless rows of channels. The children played as passionately as they worked. More than once splattering the prince and me with sludge, roots, and snail bits—to Emerys' disdain.

"And here I thought you liked the soup," I whispered as I drove my tool into the dirt.

He glanced up at me from under his lashes, wearing a cheeky smile. "Not anymore."

I grinned. "No?"

His smile widened. "If I ever see another snail in my lifetime, it will be too soon. I'll pass next time." Emerys glanced again across the flats, eyes narrowing.

Annoyed, I tried to follow his gaze. "What do you keep looking at?"

"What is that?" Emerys pointed to the stone outbuilding at the edge of the field. "It's in terrible shape."

"That?" I'd almost forgotten about it after so many years of being overgrown—it really was ugly. The roof had long collapsed, rock slabs cracked and covered in moss. "It used to be for storage back when we grew potatoes here."

Emerys cocked his head. "And now?"

"Now?" I wiped the sweat from my eyes. *I don't even want to imagine how I must look.* "It is what it is—abandoned."

Emerys leaned against his shovel. With the returning storm clouds growing on the horizon behind him, it was effortless to imagine him as a regal painting—something that would hang in the halls of the royal palace.

He asked. "Why don't you just tear it down?"

"Tear it down—" I cringed. "Papa says that it's been there since his father was young."

"And now it's useless," Emerys said, blunt. "Tear it down. Use the good materials to repair the villager's homes. Solid rock will keep them much warmer than the wood patches currently holding up their walls."

"I—" My first instinct was to argue, but slowly, a light clicked on. *That's not a bad idea.* Emerys braced for my verbal assault, sending a wave of guilt through me. Hoping to soften the moment, I smiled. "I'll talk to Papa about it." In truth, I realized, I didn't have to wait for Papa's approval—I'm his princess now—but old habits die hard, and certainly not in one night.

Smiling back, Emerys seemed to relax, but the city boy in him still struggled with his shovel. Instead of using his muscles to plunge in with deep, firm strokes, he scraped chunks off the top layer of soil, flinging it to the side. I'd noticed his poor technique hours ago but enjoyed his struggling too much to correct him.

"Stop, stop." I reached for his tool handle and missed, our hands brushing. I inhaled sharply, but neither of us recoiled. Swallowing, I gestured for him to watch. "Like this." I leaned back, using the arch of my boot to thrust the shovel blade into the dirt. Angling further, I used leverage to lift a large amount of earth and dropped it into a neat pile at the edge of our channel. "You've really never done this before?"

"Remember, I was the idea guy." After closely watching a few more times, Emerys replicated the movement perfectly.

"Better?" I asked.

He nodded. "Better."

We exchanged sheepish smiles.

It struck me then that I didn't have to be here with him. I could have wandered off to dig with the kids—or with Caddic, who'd shot me more than a few flirtatious looks throughout the afternoon.

I tried to convince myself I stayed at Emerys' side to prevent him from causing embarrassment, but what did I care if he embarrassed himself? Over and over, I repeated that thought to myself, trying to make it stick, but it wouldn't. I couldn't do it.

I watched his face as he worked, watched a contentedness settle there. *If not to spare me, then why do I stay?* I wouldn't say I liked the answer rolling around my insides.

We continued that way in silence, only interrupted by children's laughter echoing across the field. The lack of bickering made my skin itch. I couldn't take it anymore. "So," I blurted, digging for more than just soil. "How miserable are you so far? Lians is a far cry from the royal city."

"Aberaron isn't much of a prize, either," Emerys said, avoiding my actual question. "With its population, the slums, the constant activity . . . let's just say it's quieter here."

I sighed. "I wish it were quieter, still."

Emerys nodded, understanding. "The Wildmen?"

I nodded back.

"I'd heard that there were savages in the outlying territories, but I never expected them to be a problem here. Like I said before, I thought they were just a story," Emerys continued. "My father failed to inform me of the truth."

Of course, he did. "We've been fighting them for decades."

"Have they ever killed anyone?"

"My great-grandfather." I ground my teeth. "But that was years ago. They're cowards, leaning towards stealing, scavenging, and smashing everything in sight."

"Sounds to me," Emerys said, thoughtfully, "that their people are faring as poorly as yours."

"Even if," I replied stiffly, "we don't steal from others."

"Perhaps, even more poorly, then."

I didn't answer him—didn't want to admit that he might have struck a point. Everyone knew the wildness of Gwent's forests, of the Wentwood. Yet, we'd had hard years and never resorted to thieving from nearby villages. We did what we had to do to survive, but . . .

I shook my head.

"Why do you do that?"

I realized Emerys was watching me. I blinked. "Do what?"

"It's not the first time you've done it," he said. "Why do you shake your head like that?"

"Oh." My cheeks were on fire. *I never realized anyone ever noticed.* "That's how I get rid of thoughts I don't like."

Emerys gave me that cheeky grin that made my stomach tighten. "What thoughts were you running from just now, may I ask?"

I focused again on my digging, a little too intently. "None of your business."

"Would it be so bad to share that business?" Emerys asked, returning to work, as well. "Like it or not, we're husband and wife now."

I sunk my blade in the dirt, watching water pool in the hole left behind. *Would it be?* Despite my family—even though I knew they loved me—for years, I'd felt alone. Left behind as the other children grew and formed friendships . . . and more—with anyone and everyone but me.

Now here *he* was. Neither of us wanted this, but maybe . . . perhaps we could make the best of it.

No. I almost shook my head again, but I stopped myself. "You have a lot to learn, prince."

Emerys' digging speed increased dramatically after giving him the tutorial. I struggled to keep up. "I never asked," he began, eyes on the ground. "Did my arrival ruin your wedding plans to someone else?"

"No," I straightened. Not once had that thought crossed my mind. "It didn't, and why ask now? A little late for that, don't you think?"

Emerys didn't answer immediately, but I saw the way his eyes flashed to the top of the hill, straight to where Caddic stood talking with Drystan. *When did my brother arrive?* The two of them strode away, out of view. Drystan had probably convinced Caddic to help him rebuild his snail pen.

A flicker of warmth rippled through me, and I smiled. "Why?"

Emerys shrugged. "Just curious."

"Did you have anyone?"

"No."

"At least that's one thing we have in common."

Voice strained, Emerys continued. "We may find that we have much more—" When he didn't continue, I looked up to see his eyes widen, locked onto the forest.

"What is it—" I realized then what caught his attention, and my blood turned to ice in my veins.

Four Wildmen stood on the edge of the tree line—just watching us, crouched—three young and one old. Instinctually, I grabbed Emerys' elbow and let out a two-note whistle. The children screamed as they realized the danger and began sprinting back toward the village.

I snagged the eldest's sleeve as he passed, turning him toward me. "Alert the others," I whispered, and he nodded, face filled with terror. "Now."

The elder Wildmen took a step toward us, intimidating in his deer-skin clothing, rusted knife in his hands. Now that I had a closer look, he couldn't be much older than forty, aged by his wild, unkempt beard and sun-browned skin.

Beside me, Emerys trembled. I squeezed his elbow tighter, voice low as I said. "Do you have a weapon under that pretty cloak?"

Emerys looked at me, sucking in a few deep breaths before he smiled. "Yes, but it's not in my . . . cloak." Before I could respond, Emerys spread his arms wide, striding toward the Wildmen, the picture of ease and confidence. "Hello, friends! How may I be of service?"

As you can imagine, my jaw dropped.

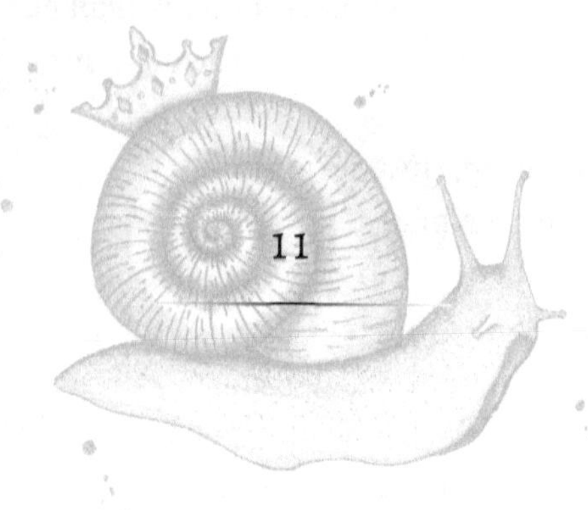

11

"A smooth, bruised talker."

ord in Heaven, what is happening right now?
The Wildmen probably wondered the same thing. They exchanged nervous glances as Emerys approached, their bodies shifting into a defensive position.

"My friends, how has this fair-weather treated you?" Emerys beamed. "I didn't think it possible for so much water to fall from the sky until I arrived in Gwent."

Despite the leaden horror filling my limbs, I forced myself to follow him, to—protect him? *Again, why do I care? If they kill him, I'll be free. Free and unconsummated.* My stomach rolled, a mix of confusion, guilt, and fear. The image of his sweet, nervous smile flashed across my mind—the way he watched me from under his lashes, the iciness of his eyes.

I can't believe I'm doing this. I rushed forward, focused on the Wildmen, looping my arm through Emerys' and pulling him tightly against me. "What do you think you're doing?"

Emerys leaned over and whispered in my ear. The Wildmen would just see the gesture as just a sweet nothing. "Stalling. Negotiating. Please, *try* and trust me for once."

Our eyes locked—his stubbornness matching my own. Slowly, I lowered my gaze. "You're a mad milksop, you know that?"

He gave me a weak smile before turning back to the very confused and agitated looking men, replacing his mask of confidence, shifting from a smiling boy to a prince.

All at once, the realization struck me like Caddic's hammer.

It's a *mask.*

The harsh words he spoke the night of the raid, the stagnant expressions, the boldness with people who insulted him—all a front.

Just like the one he wore now.

But why? Our marriage was merely a way for the King to extort gold from Lians—the prince a constant reminder that my father's deadline would soon be up. *But who does Emerys have to impress? He's a prince.*

But the *sixth* in line to the throne. Unless all his brothers died, one by one, he'd never truly wear a crown. Our entire lives, Drystan never let me live it down that he's three minutes older. How must it feel to have five siblings shove that fact down your throat, day after day?

Pain fluttered through my heart, but I chased it away. Now wasn't a great time for a sentimental moment. Maybe later, if we survived, I'd come back to this thought and give it proper attention.

As Emerys stopped—mere feet from the Wildmen—despite all the years of hate and bitterness, against the anger coiled inside me, I gave the intruders my widest, sweetest smile.

I could nearly taste the tension rolling off the four men. I must not look very convincing, probably more like a wolf on the hunt. I jumped as Emerys gave my arm a gentle squeeze, but I understood his message. *Play this part with me.*

We were close enough to see the color of the men's eyes—blues, greens, and browns. I could see the veins bulging in their temples, the twitch flickering in the eldest's jaw.

Emerys grinned, dipping his chin respectfully. "What brings you today, friends?"

Another glance between them. The eldest gestured toward the flats behind us, the breeze dusting his thinning curls over his narrow face. "We were near," he began, voice surprisingly gentle. "Smelled the tilled earth. Wondered why you lot were digging so many holes in our ground."

"*Your* ground?" I bristled.

Emerys reached out and took my hand, squeezing it before pressing it to his lips. A warning. "We're creating drainage channels to keep the crops from drowning in the future rains. Would you like to have a look at our methods?"

I didn't miss the way the elder one studied the contact between us. He pointed a scarred, thin finger at me, and I snapped my teeth at him in response. "Her, I know," he said. "The crippled mayor's big daughter."

"*Big?*" I blurted angrily.

He ignored me, shifting his accusing finger to Emerys. "But I don't know you. You the new prince everyone is talking about? We hope you enjoyed your party. We sure did."

Cowardly, dim-witted chicken leg—

Emerys bowed deeply, jerking me down with him. "I am. Again, how can I be of service?"

I pinched the inside of his arm and whispered. "Don't make any offers."

Emerys winked at me. More feigned confidence.

The eldest broke into deep, heady chuckles—the younger Wildmen followed suit. If I had a sword, I would have gutted them right then and there. The elder cocked his head, smirking.

"Oh, that fur you're wearing would make a fine gift for my wife. I wonder how many nights she'd have me for it if you get my meaning."

The Wildmen howled in laughter.

Mimicking their laughs, Emerys shrugged off his cloak along the fine wool doublet he wore beneath, leaving him in only his damp undershirt. Despite his gangliness, Emerys carried more muscle than I expected.

He tossed the clothing to the elder Wildmen, who caught it with ease. Eyes wide, the man ran his rough fingers through the fur, callused skin catching on the thick wool. Before the prince arrived, I'd never seen fabrics so grand. I couldn't imagine how beautiful they must be to this savage.

The man eyed Emerys suspiciously, who just smiled in return and said, "A token of understanding, from one deprived husband to another."

Again, a roar of laughter escaped the Wildmen as a wave of heat burned through me.

The laughter died as shouting began behind us.

Oh no, not now. Cringing, I turned. Papa, Drystan, Caddic—every able man in the village barreled down the hill with whatever weapons they could find—hunks of wood, fire pokers, a carriage spoke. Papa froze on the edge of the flats, unable to traverse the muck with his pegleg. His eyes locked onto mine, mouthing something I couldn't understand.

I couldn't show weakness, not now, nor could I let them ruin the impossible progress Emerys had made. Steeling myself, I raised my hand as the mob approached, putting on the same confident mask Emerys wore. "Wait," I called, loudly, stern.

To my infinite relief, they stopped. Midway through the flats, Drystan's eyes narrowed, asking me a silent question. *What are you playing at?*

I answered back with my own stare, hoping he understood. *Trust me.*

Trust me, like I'd chosen to trust Emerys.

When I turned back, the Wildmen had drawn their crude weapons and looked, dare I say, fearful. Hands raised in good faith, Emerys stepped closer. "These years have been hard, haven't they? Your people are hurting?"

One of the younger men spat directly onto Emerys' boot. "What do you care? You don't know hurt, princeling."

Emerys paused, deep in thought. "You're right, I don't—and to be honest, I *didn't* care."

I kept still. *I'm trusting you. What's your plan, my dear, stupid husband?*

Emerys continued, "A lot has changed for me recently. Not always pleasantly, but it has. I'd like to change things for you, as well."

The younger Wildmen returned Emerys' steps, closing the distance between them. Besides my fear, I could feel the village men behind me about to explode with rage.

When the man was in touching distance, I considered dragging the prince away by the ear, scolding him for being such a fool, but a sick sense of curiosity stopped me.

The Wildmen leaned in as if he meant to whisper into Emerys' ear. "What can you do for us, you ask?" His voice only loud enough so his group and I could hear. A thrill of fear ran through me as he gripped Emerys' shoulder and muttered. "You can shove off."

So fast—so, so fast—the Wildmen rammed his knee into Emerys' groin—the impact hard enough I winced.

Emerys keeled over, mouth gaping, but no noise escaped. I tried to catch him, but he hit the ground, curling around himself. Another wave of laughter rolled through the Wildmen, but when I looked over, the elder seemed upset.

I heard Drystan scream. "Kill them!"

The Wildmen sprinted into the forest as the mob surged after them, moving around us. I shook Emerys' shoulder and realized he'd vomited. "You have to get up." I shook him again, and he groaned. "You can't let them get away with this. Get up!"

When he finally glanced up at me, tears rolled down his cheeks. From the pain—they must be from the pain.

I backed away. *Please, don't expect me to comfort you. I'm terrible at this.*

When he finally got to his feet, I found myself wanting to—wanting to tell him that he'd been brave—stupid, but brave. That I didn't care that his balls probably now resided in between his kidneys. Not knowing what else to do, I reached out for him—

And Emerys pulled away. Turning, he began his slow limp back toward the castle.

It would be a long walk, and I didn't dare follow him. Part of me knew he wouldn't want me to.

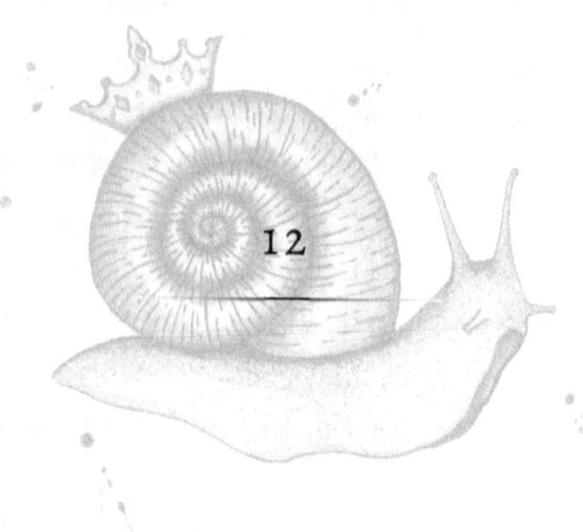

12

"Thicker than the water of the womb."

"**A**re you sure you've tried everything?"

Sweet Wynny. Even though the rain remained merely a drizzle, she huddled deep into the hood of her thick cloak. I paused, wiping the moisture mixed with sweat from my brow. I huffed. "Yes, *everything.*"

Even if I had to do it alone, I would finish the drains we'd started on the mudflats. Soil and water would not defeat me. Six days after the most recent Wildmen incident, I'd almost finished digging the retention pond.

The blisters on my fingers bled through their bandages. Getting out of bed in the morning was excruciating from my back and shoulders stiffness, but I couldn't stop. Not until I finished—I owed Emerys that much.

Wynny stood at the edge of the ten-foot-wide hole, watching me, rocking from foot to foot to keep warm. "What about an apology basket?"

I scoffed, tossing out a shovel full of dirt. "I've never heard of an apology basket."

"You know," Wynny smiled, hazel eyes bright against the grey sky. "It's when you get all the person's favorite things and arrange them in a basket. You leave it somewhere for them to find with an apology letter."

Okay, that's enough. I dropped my shovel, surveying my makeshift pond. *This will have to do.* Struggling to climb out, Wynny offered me her hand. I wiped my muddy hands on my trouser legs. "No, I did not leave him an *apology basket.* I have nothing to apologize for."

Wynny scowled, an odd expression for her usually cheerful face. *She doesn't believe that any more than I do.* "Even if," she huffed. "It might be a nice gesture."

Sighing, I plopped down on the damp grass, laying back so the mist could cool my overheated skin. Six days since the incident, and I hadn't seen him once—even when I'd tried to. I blew out a breath. "I've gone to his rooms three times, and there's no answer. The fourth time I tried, Catrin threatened to beat me with the broomstick she flies on."

Wynny giggled. "She doesn't have a broomstick."

I rolled my eyes. "You know what I mean."

Wynny kneeled, brushing the grass with her gloved hand before she sat, as if that would keep her bottom from getting wet. "*Oh.*" She leaned toward me, shielding her mouth. "You were calling her a witch, but I think what you really meant was—"

"Language, young lady!" I feigned a gasp, and we burst into giggles. As the laughter subsided, sadness returned to fill its place. I placed my hands behind my head. "I don't know what else I can do. I've attended every meal in the main hall, and he hasn't come. I've walked the grounds. Waited in the kitchens and libraries. Emerys doesn't want to see me."

Wynny didn't say anything, just patted my arm gently.

I'd tried to go to him that first night.

The village mob chased the Wildmen into the forest, only to find that they'd vanished—absorbed into the ferns and pine, not a trace left behind. I waited in the tree line, chewing my nails down to the point of bleeding until my brother returned.

Of course, he was spitting mad—demanding to know what I'd been thinking, if the prince was insane, if I was insane. I didn't have an answer for him.

That night, every step felt tied down with boulders as I climbed the staircase toward Emerys' suite. When I arrived, I found the door locked and the lights out, and I cried every step back down, from the pain in my body—and I hated to admit—the pain in my heart.

I tried the following day, and the morning after that—nothing. By the end of the third day, my pity had waned, being replaced by irritation and a wounded ego. The man I'd seen standing before the Wildmen, fighting for peace, must just have been a dream. A second mask behind the one I'd already discovered. Only a coward would hide from his wife.

Like you hid from him?

I shook the thought away, and Wynny's dramatic sigh snapped me back from my thoughts. She wrapped her arms around herself, nose bright pink.

Groaning, I climbed to my feet. I shouldn't have kept her out so long. Shouldn't have asked her to come at all, but I didn't want to be alone. Lately, my thoughts were too pervasive to be by myself for long. I grabbed her hand and helped her up—at her full height, she still only came to my shoulders.

"Come on." I tossed my tools over my shoulder, taking her hand with my free one. "Let's take these back to Caddic."

"The blacksmith?" Wynny grinned. "Oh, I've heard a lot about *him*." When my brow rose, she added. "I hear the other women whisper." She placed her hand over her heart. "And you called *my* language bad. Oi. Their curses could curl the crotch hairs on a fly!"

"You called your own language bad," I replied, shaking my head. "I merely encouraged your behavior."

Chuckling, we headed up the hill together as she shared just how terrible the other women really were, and I found myself quite enlightened.

A short time later, we reached the blacksmith. The leather straps covering the door to Caddic's shop were pinned open when we arrived, most likely to let the heat building inside escape into the cool autumn afternoon. Wynny held onto me tightly, face pinched as we entered. Caddic stood in the corner of his shop, an elaborately decorated package on the table in front of him.

I knocked the shovel blade against the wall to get his attention. "Just returning these."

He nodded, attention fixed on the package. Wynny pulled against me as I moved towards him. "What's in the box?" I asked.

Finally, Caddic's gaze moved in my direction but strayed to Wynny, still clinging to my side. His lips curled up into a smile I knew all too well as his eyes passed over her from head to toe— a man on the hunt.

Wynny turned her attention to the floor. Clearing his throat, Caddic gestured to the package, remembering himself. "Look for yourself."

Cautiously, I moved to the table and peeked inside—a hand-carved hammer lay wrapped inside on a silk cushion. I scowled. *What's this about?* Its handle was sanded and polished to perfection, engraved with a snail. The steel pure and clean—more beautiful than I'd ever seen in my life. I stepped back, shocked. Caddic rubbed the stubble growing along his jaw, and I realized his eyes were red and puffy.

"From who?" I asked, stunned, but I already knew the answer.

Caddic passed me a note. "This was inside."

I took the note, fingers trembling, and read: *The best I could do on short notice. Thanks for digging.*

The hammer wouldn't be used as a weapon, wouldn't be used to hurt—but to build. Repair. Grow.

My own throat tightened as I fought back tears. I nodded to Caddic. "Enjoy your new toy." I couldn't stand to look at it any longer. The door's leather straps snapped across my cheeks as I pushed out of the hut. Wynny whimpered something behind me, but I ignored her.

As I headed out into the fresh rain, she grabbed my wrist, hazel eyes filled with concern. "What's wrong, Rhia? Talk to me."

I wheeled on her, breathing heavily. "I can't keep up with the plots and ruses. What's he after? Emerys can afford that steel but can't pay Lians' debts? Does that seem right to you?"

"Why don't you ask him?" Wynny crossed her arms, moisture building on the fur of her cloak.

I grabbed her shoulders. "That's what he wants! He wants me to break first, I know it. I can't figure out how to fight it. Papa wants so much, I—"

A streak of pain rippled across my cheek. Appalled, I held my face, staring up at Wynny's flushed face shifting between panic and resolve. *She slapped me!*

Wynny blinked down at her open hand. "Huh," she hesitated. "You could put me to death for that."

I stuttered. "You know I never would."

She sucked in a breath. "Is it so unbelievable to think that a person can do a kind thing for another without an ulterior motive?"

It took a moment to collect myself. "Not him. With anyone but him, maybe, but—"

I never knew I needed something so much until Wynny pulled me into a hug. I let out an ugly sob into her shoulder as her arms wrapped around my waist. "I can't fix this." I shuddered into the dampness of her cloak. "They think I can fix this, but I can't. What's going to happen to Lians if I fail?"

Wynny patted my hair, used her fingers to comb through the tangles. "The real question should be, what would happen if you took care of yourself first? Forget them. Forget them all. What do you want?"

Think of myself first? Have I ever done that? Even when I was small, I did everything possible to see Mama and Papa smile. Even if that meant waking hours earlier than the rest of the house to finish the chores before daybreak or spending my childhood in the shadow of what Drystan would become—a mayor, and I'd just be his oversized, wild sister. Useless beyond brood stock, that's how the young men in the village saw the women. Only there to cook, clean, raise children, and spread their legs when asked.

"Is that a problem?" I'd asked Emerys, back in his suite. It felt like ages ago.

"Not to me," He'd said. Had he meant that? I remembered what Catrin said. *"You'll come to appreciate a man that heeds the words of the women in his life."* Is this what she meant?

Wynny's anchor kept me grounded to the shore.

I breathed out, and she released her grip, tears mixing with the rain that dripped down her creamy cheeks. I wiped my eyes. *I can't believe I cried like that in front of her.* I wiped my running nose, heading back toward the road. I needed to think. "C'mon. We still need to grab a few things for Papa."

Wynny just nodded as she caught up to my side, laying her head on my shoulder as we stepped back into the rain, arm in arm.

———

Wynny's skin turned a novel shade of green as the butcher's knife thudded into his cutting table.

I hated to say, but the butcher, Derfel . . . there was no uglier man you'd ever meat—I mean, meet. Though not much older than Caddic, his mousy hair had thinned around the crown. Having decided to grow instead on his back, where it peeked over the collar of his shirt. He'd never made any advances on the village girls. I suspected that he preferred sheep, but they weren't ones to gossip. His blade slammed through the hip joints of the lamb in front of him, separating it from the torso.

His voice crawled across my skin like a leech. Another crack of knife through bone. "Does your father want his usual cut?"

"As always," I said, counting out ten pennies. He snatched them out of my palm without hesitation. The way his roof leaked—not just in droplets, but full streams—I understood. Derfel's knife came down again, and Wynny's face shifted from green to colorless. He trimmed and wrapped our cut of meat, passing it over without a word. I dropped it into my shopping bag and pulled up my hood, ready to head back into the sour weather.

"Funny finding you here."

I turned to the familiar voice I knew better than my own—Drystan—and smiled. "You're just jealous I got here first. Won't Papa be pleased with me when he sees this hunk of deliciousness."

He smiled back, but I realized it wasn't for me. The width of my brother's grin could have brought a kingdom to its knees—and the full force of it was focused in on Wynny. Not in the same way Caddic looked at her—like a wolf about to take down a deer—but like a child experiencing snow for the first time, pure wonder.

Drystan snorted and winked at Wynny—who, instead of hiding, blushed. "Me, jealous? You're sorely mistaken, dear sister."

"Aren't you?" I quipped

"It would be petty to be jealous of someone who came into the world so much later than I. Of someone who doesn't have the life experience, the aptitude."

"Kiss my bunions," I snarled. Wynny subtlety cleared her throat, prodding my elbow with her own. Pulling her closer against me, echoes of our hug still in reach, I grinned. "Brother, have you met my handmaid, Wynny? I wouldn't have survived without her these last weeks."

Wynny's let out that shrill squeal—unable to contain herself —as Drystan bowed, taking her hand in his and kissing her knuckles. I wanted to gag. "I haven't had the honor. I am so pleased to meet you, my lady."

Instead of pulling away, as I expected, Wynny's cheeks flushed a brilliant pink as she did everything possible to hold back a grin of her own. "The honor is mine." Breathless, she dipped into a flawless curtsy.

I glanced between them. *Am I imagining this?*

"So," Drystan smoothed his coat, then rubbed his hands together briskly. "What are you ladies up to on this fine day, besides running Papa's errands? Strolling?" He glanced at my bag. "Shopping? Lians doesn't have much in the way of merchandise, but we do have quite the assortment of fixer-upper homes available."

Before I could answer, Wynny quipped with her sing-song voice. "Rhia finished digging the retention pond." She beamed at me proudly. "I bet you can grow all the potatoes in the world now."

"Ah, really." Drystan shot me a look, which I understood loud and clear. *Why are you helping him?*

I returned his look with equal venom. *I'm not. Mind your own business.*

I just want what's best for you.

I doubt that.

Drystan recoiled, backing away a step. Confused, Wynny's gaze flickered between the two of us. I looped my arm through hers and gave my brother one of my signature croons. "I'll be delivering this to Papa. Care to join?"

Tension forgotten—or maybe it was just the hormones—Drystan grinned again. "Will Lady Wynny be walking with us?"

"Oh, yes." Wynny squeezed my hand. "I would love to see your childhood home, Rhia."

"It's not much, but it is, indeed, a home." Drystan started, and before I knew it, Wynny was on his arm instead of mine. "I built a good portion of it myself. Rhia helped, of course." Drystan paused, turning to look Wynny fully in the eyes, and said in a painfully tragic voice. "My lady, do you like snails?"

Lord Almighty. I rolled my eyes.

Wynny burst into giggles, then covered her mouth shyly. "To be honest, I don't know much about them."

"I—" Drystan chewed his lip, brushing gold curls from his eyes. "I keep some as pets. Would you like to see the palace I built for them? I imagine it rivals Aberaron itself."

Dear, precious Lord, spare me.

"Would I?" Wynny gasped. "How sweet! I would love to see."

I'd never seen anything more heart wrenching than the glorious, genuine smile that spread on my brother's face—or the equally beautiful one Wynny gave him in return.

The entire walk back to our hut, they walked arm and arm, shoulders brushing, the conversation never lagging.

I kept pace behind them, a heaviness building in my chest with every step. *Why does this bother me?* Why did their giggles sound so irritating? Why did watching them touch make me want to physically pull them apart and drag Wynny back to the castle?

She's *my* friend—the only one I had.

Drystan didn't have to be dragged from his home to marry a stranger. Why did *he* get to choose whom he liked?

An image of Emerys and I walking together in the courtyard played through my mind, hand in hand, smiling and laughing. Happy, warm, safe. *Could it have been possible?*

My eyes stung as I shook the thought away. Best not dwell on what would never be.

As our hut came into view, I sighed in relief at the sight of smoke rising from the chimney. The smell of Mama's home-made bread leaked from the closed shudders, making my mouth water.

To the left of the front door, a new construction replaced Drystan's smashed snail house. This new emporium stood at least three feet tall and equally wide, branches and twigs peeking over the top. Drystan gestured towards it, and Wynny squealed in excitement. She turned to me. "Rhia, hurry, let's go have a look!"

I did my best to smile, but the way hers fell proved that mine wasn't so convincing. "You go on ahead. I'll give Papa his package."

She nodded, bright energy returning as she and Drystan trotted off to see his snails, making the heaviness inside near unbearable as I pushed inside my family's hut.

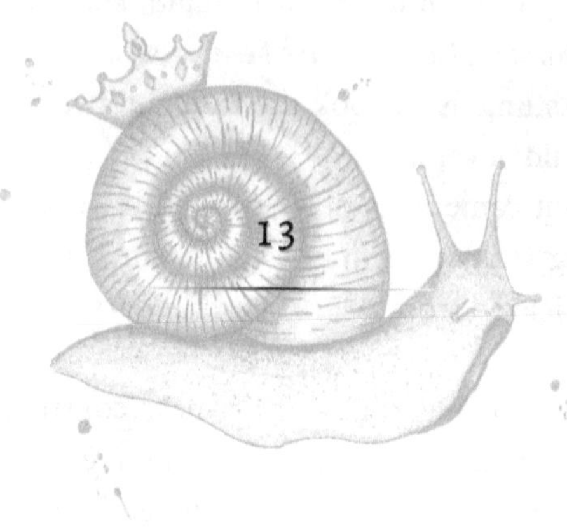

13

"Old wounds run deep."

I hadn't seen Papa since the night of the incident. Thanks to Drystan, word of Emerys' "injury" got around—*fast*. Fortunately, no one tried to talk to me about it yet, or *their* balls would have wound up in their throats.

Wynny and Drystan had spent the afternoon playing with his snails while I helped Mama cook. By the time they'd come inside, Wynny's skin flushed and smelling of fresh air, she'd never looked so beautiful. Instead of her usual ornate gown, she wore a simpler dress beneath her cloak. Less constricting, less decoration. Instead of a tight updo, her curls lay braided over her shoulder. She looked so much more . . . free.

Now we all sat together at my parent's cramped dining table. It didn't surprise me that Mama took so well to Wynny. They'd met before, but now seeing them together, she could be a second daughter to Mama—whimsical, generous, and a heart made of gold.

I wasn't sure how that made me feel.

Papa dug into his salt marsh lamb—a dish only available to us in the late summer and fall. Blowing on the morsel coating his fork, he said. "I saw what you did in the flats. Good work. I'd like to have the rest done by spring."

Coward. I glanced up from my plate. Just like him to avoid bringing up the Wildmen. For all his tough talk with others, he'd always avoided conflict with me—we were too much alike. So, I just nodded, picking apart my lamb.

"I haven't seen it myself, but I hear there's already a great improvement in the soil." Mama chipped in, always so pleasant. "I look forward to seeing what rewards your hard work will sow, Rhia."

"It wasn't my idea," I said flatly. Wynny gave me an anxious look, but I did my best to avoid it. *They're all worried about me. Probably afraid I'm about to ruin their dreams for Lians.*

Papa's voice interrupted my thoughts. "Have you seen him at all?"

Shaking my head, I forced myself to take a bite of lamb. It tasted like dirt. "No. Good riddance."

Papa glanced up and down the table before leaning in close, face reddening. "Is he injured . . . down there? I'd hoped for grandchildren, but—"

I slammed my goblet down, spilling milk across my plate.

Papa quickly returned to his meal, sweat dripping down his temples. Drystan snorted behind his hand. I arched my brow. "Do you have something cute to say, as well?"

Grinning lazily, he replied. "Not at all." I hadn't missed the way his eyes never trailed far from Wynny during the evening. He took a bite of bread, but after another minute, he burst into another fit of giggles, spewing crumbs on the table runner.

Gritting my teeth, I tried to ignore him until Papa said. "And you know, tax time is coming soon. I hoped—"

I stood, the chair legs scraping too loud as my hips hit the table. Without another word, I marched from the hut, out into the chill of the evening. From inside, I heard Mama scolding Papa and Drystan.

They wouldn't follow me. They knew better.

The sun had set, casting the rare clear sky in golds, and I sucked in a deep breath. It did little—I couldn't get the storm inside me to calm. Before I'd gone ten feet, I heard soft footsteps approaching. Wynny reached my elbow, stalking beside me. I glanced over, expecting pity or annoyance, but instead, her groomed brows arched.

I looked away. "Can I help you?"

The poor thing had to jog to keep up with my long stride. "You're going to see the prince, aren't you?"

I nodded. We continued along the trail back toward the heart of the village.

After ten minutes of silence, Wynny let out a sharp breath to get my attention. "You know, if you really want to apologize to him, I could teach you how to—"

I swatted her arm, cheeks burning like biscuits straight from the oven. "I am *not* apologizing."

Wynny shrugged, smiling at my expression. "As you wish, princess."

As we passed Town Hall, I realized she was still smiling. I smirked. "Why so toothy?"

It was Wynny's turn to blush as she cuddled deeper into her cloak. "It's just . . . your brother is quite attractive."

I snorted, which seemed to startle her. "You can have him."

"I—but you are—" Wynny blinked, then that cheeky smile returned. "He does stare at me often, doesn't he?"

I rolled my eyes. "He likes your *assets*."

She glanced down at the low neckline she wore beneath her outer layers, then shrugged again. "I don't blame him."

Despite my foul mood, we burst into laughter. It echoed through the darkness all the way back to the castle. When we reached the main entry, Wynny waved goodnight, heading toward her rooms in my tower.

As longingly as bed called for me, I turned for the East Wing, trekking up the tower staircase toward the prince's rooms. Sweat dripped down my sides, chafing my underarms. *What if he's not there? What if I can't fix this?* I hated how much I thought about him. How his face, his laugh, his low voice consumed my waking moments. *I barely know him. I shouldn't care.*

But I did. For some tiresome, unknown reason—I did. I would try again, one more time. He'd earned that much.

When I passed the last landing, a shadowy lump blocked my path—Catrin. Eyes narrowing, she rubbed her bony knuckles, scowling at me.

How did she know I'd be here? Maybe I was wrong. She is a dragon. I kept my voice even. "And you call me the spy. What are you doing here?"

"I could ask the same of you." The older woman clamored to her feet, using the railing to brace herself. She dusted some wood shavings off her apron. "Come to make a fool of yourself again?"

"Me—" I began, but she cut me off.

"First the bloody ceremony," Catrin growled. "Then the fields. Don't you dare come here and—"

"That's enough." Emerys' voice was so low—cold—as he cracked open his door. Eyes shadowed purple, skin sallow. "I'm going to have to ask you not to speak to my wife that way."

Catrin bowed her head but shot me a look that could kill a badger. I held her stare as she passed me, held it until she had to turn her back as she slowly headed down the steep staircase.

Any hope I might have had disappeared as I turned back, taking in Emerys expression—it even more frigid than his voice, then the same bored look he wore at our wedding returned. "Can I help you?"

Doesn't that sound familiar. Even though I'd tried to convince myself that it didn't matter, that I didn't care—his demeanor punched me deep in the gut. "Do I need a reason to visit?"

Without a word, Emerys strode back into his suite, leaving the door open. As I entered behind him, he slid into his desk chair, crossing his legs as he returned to his papers.

I glanced around. The room hadn't changed—his bags still lay unpacked, sheets still covered some of the furniture. He hadn't personalized anything.

When it was clear he wouldn't be acknowledging me, I sighed. "Why haven't I seen you around? You've been hiding for days."

Emerys shot me a brief glare. "I wasn't hiding."

"Then what do you call it?"

He continued digging through his papers, searching for something. "Mimicking you, perhaps. If I remember correctly, you've done a wonderful job avoiding me these last weeks."

I didn't know what to say.

Finally, he found what he was looking for. Emerys held out a neatly folded letter. "I've also been busy with this. Since I don't know when I'll see you next, I best show you now."

Run. Run. Run. But I couldn't. Trembling, I took the note from him, throat tight as I opened it—the script neat and absurdly small. As my eyes scanned over the letters, my heart stopped, sputtered, then tried to break free of my ribs as it slammed in my chest.

I've had enough of these filthy peasant games. Expect a host within a fortnight from this raven's arrival. I have nothing else to say to you.

You've disappointed me,
King Beyron—

Crumpling the letter, I threw it into the fire burning in his hearth. "When did you get this?"

Emerys' face remained emotionless. "The day of we started on the field."

A week ago. I took everything I had not to tear his head from his shoulders. I sucked in a breath, jaw clenched. "You've known this long and haven't told anyone? Told me? He can't do this. He never gave us time—"

"He can, and he will," Emerys scowled. "Lians has avoided the consequences of its actions for far too long."

"We are our own people." I choked through the tightness in my throat. "We have been since Lians' founding. We've survived through conditions that others would have died under."

"*We—*" Emerys interrupted sharply. "—Are a people under the rule of the King of Wales. Lians is *years* in debt to its monarch. If *we* do not pay, my father will remove Lians from the map and give the land to someone that will pay."

This.

This is what I expected when Papa came to me in the night, the letter clutched in his fist when he told me I'd be marrying a prince—a rotten, arrogant son of a heifer.

"Fix it," I growled, low, venomous. "Isn't that why you came? To prove to your rich court friends that you can push around a bunch of insolent degenerates?"

A range of emotions passed over Emerys features before settling on a wave of calm anger. He stood. "You are exactly like my father, aren't you?"

I took a step back. "Excuse me?"

"She warned me." Emerys shook his head. "Catrin—but I didn't believe her. I was wrong. You take pleasure in tearing people down, just like him—and just like him, you demand and expect the impossible. Force Lians to pay. Save the village. Stop the Wildmen. Appease the King. You demand, but whenever I try, all you do is humiliate me. The court . . . the villagers, what difference does it make?"

Just like that, my heart broke.

Breathing heavily, I wrang my hands as Emerys returned to his desk. As he picked up his pen, he glanced up at me, bored. "Is there anything else?"

I watched him for a moment, pieces falling apart before I turned and strode from the room.

I ran from one end of the castle to the other, tears streaming down my cheeks. I tried to hide them, but I knew that servants saw, that they'd start whispering.

You're exactly like my father.

My entire life, all I'd heard was my father's complaints about the King. That Lians would never bow to such a man. That if he wanted his blood money, he could come to get it himself. And from the moment Papa revealed the news of my betrothal, all I heard was how I must sway the prince to change the King's mind.

I'd never given Emerys—Emerys the person—a chance.

He had tried, done kind things for me—and all I'd done is stomp him down at every turn.

And now the King was coming, and there was nothing I could do to stop him.

I swooped into my suite and locked the doors behind me. Jacc lay curled on the foot of my bed. His head rose, and he meowed at my sobs. I curled up around him, his fur sticking to my wet cheeks. Wynny, Mama, Catrin—everyone knew how terrible I'd been.

In the window sill sat my yellow rose. Wynny had kept it watered instead of letting it die as I would have—because I'd been too selfish to see its beauty. Two more blooms had joined the originals. It really was beautiful, filling the room with its sweet scent.

Jacc purred as I stroked his coat. He'd gained weight of royal table scraps. How long would the food Emerys brought from Aberaron last? Would we even make it until winter, or would the King indeed destroy Lians, just like that?

As I ran my hand along the length of Jacc's tail, something sticking out of my blankets scratched my elbow.

I sat up, wiping my eyes. A small scrap of paper lay on my bed. Inside, I recognized the handwriting as Wynny's. She'd written only one word: *Apologize.*

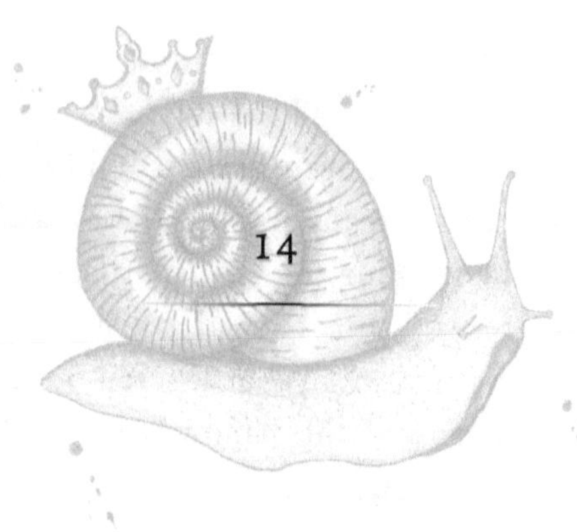

14

"Wise words in uncomfortable places."

Before dawn, I was on my way to Mama's and Papa's.

I moved painfully slow, putting too much thought into each step as I moved through the village's empty streets. Faces watched me from their windows, but I didn't care. My joints ached, muscles in my back stiff from crying. I probably looked like a ghost.

I'd tossed and turned all night, stewing over Wynny's note, about words said. I'd never felt more like a worm—dirty, slimy, and barely inching through life. Would my back end keep on living if I was sliced in half? Could I grow a new head?

I'd treated Emerys like garbage—I'd accepted that—and possibly doomed Lians in the process. Could we have already come up with a solution to the taxes if I'd just listened, allowed us to work together? If I'd appreciated his knowledge of politics? Something I completely lacked.

Either way, if the note was truthful, the King's men would be here within the week.

As I trudged down the road, a tiny bit of golden sunlight peeked through the heavy clouds, reflecting light through the drizzling rain. Hopefully, we'd have a rainbow soon—a promise of the Lord's goodness. If only I could repair mine.

Despite the dampness, the day felt muggy. I closed my eyes, letting the mist cool me. It did nothing for my racing thoughts. What happened to a village when none of its people remained? Would the King give Lians to someone else, like Emerys mentioned? Would it sit and rot—buildings collapsing in on themselves as time wore stone to dust?

More importantly, what would happen to us? I doubted we'd be invited to Aberaron. We'd probably have to beg a neighboring village to take us in, even though the nearest was thirty miles away and more petite than Lians—and in even worse shape. There's no way any of them could afford more mouths to feed.

I shook my head—a week. I had a week.

Even in such tiny morsels, the caress of the sun's rays on my skin felt heavenly as it burnt through the rain. I passed through the village, savoring the sound of the children's laughter as they played in fresh puddles. Another week and they'd be gone.

I missed summer days. Missed the warm, heavy night air kissing my neck and bare calves. No one here cared about rules or formalities, wouldn't care if I ran around in my underclothes as long as I was helpful when needed. Drystan and I often went on nighttime adventures when we were young—collecting fireflies, searching for sleeping wildflowers to bring home to Mama. Papa would wink at us and pretend he'd done all the work of picking them when we'd present our haul.

Drystan—I needed him. We hadn't been the same since the wedding. Since Papa had announced the wedding, really. I missed him, missed Mama and Papa. Missed my tiny hut and straw mattress. Missed cold morning curled under my torn blankets, listening to the kettle whistling as Mama boiled it over the stove.

Had Emerys ever sat curled in *his* mama's arms, sipping tea on a cold morning? Had his papa ever read him stories by the fire?

Throat tight, I rubbed my chest. My heart hurt—for him, for myself, for what I'd done. I wanted Mama.

Several of the villagers waved at me as I passed into the outskirts, and I managed to smile back.

Like the night before, smoke still danced lazily from my family's chimney—thank goodness. My feet were soddened. The idea of stripping off my wet socks and letting my toes warm by the fire sounded exquisite.

I pushed the front door, letting it swing open on its squeaky, repaired hinges—then screamed.

Mama's head popped up from between Papa's legs. He sat sprawled on a chair beside the dining table, eyes bugged at the sight of me. After glancing between us, Mama rolled her eyes, waving a razor. "Relax." Mama was shaving Papa's upper thigh.

I crept around the edge of the table, nearly in a panic attack. I placed my hand over my chest. "Lord Almighty."

"You think you'd be used to such intimate duties," Drystan said, stepping out of the bedroom, a plate of cheese and bread in his hands. "You know, being a married woman and all."

Papa shuddered. "Please, don't remind me. *Ack.*"

Mama slapped Papa's thigh, and he yelped. "Quiet, you toad, or I'll cut your artery."

Drystan sat at the table. Nauseous, I sat beside him, watching Mama work the razor with quick even precision. Drystan offered me a bit of cheese, and I brushed it away, bile rising in my throat. It burned as I swallowed it down. "Mama, *why* are you doing that?"

"Because," Mama drawled, setting down the blade. She

wiped Papa's leg off with a damp towel, smiling up at him. "Shaving helps the wrap beneath his false leg fit more comfortably."

I never thought of that. Shuddering, I replied, "That's disgusting." Then I nodded to Papa. "No offense."

He glowered at me, wincing as Mama rewrapped his leg. She gave me a stern look, but I could see the amusement behind them. "What do you think love is, Rhi-Rhi?"

I wrinkled my nose. "Combing body hair?"

Drystan snorted, and Mama rolled her eyes again. "*No.*" She stood, straightening her plaid skirt. "Love is self-sacrifice. As disgusting as *body hair* may be, if it makes Papa more comfortable, I'll do it, no question."

"But why can't he just do it?"

"He could, but I have steadier hands."

I bite off a chunk of Drystan's bread just to give me something to do as I thought. Mama had always been so good, caring. More loving than anyone I'd ever known—not like me. My heart sank. Cupping my chin, I said. "It doesn't matter. I've ruined things with Emerys."

Papa strapped on his wooden leg. "It's only been two weeks!"

"Oh, you!" Mama swatted him again, then turned to me. "What makes you say that?"

The words felt like acid as I spoke. "The king's men will be here by the end of the week. Either we pay or leave."

One by one, horror passed over their faces. Followed by defiance, then despair. Papa slumped in his chair, dropping his head into his hands. Mama just stared blankly across the room, rubbing his shoulder.

"I cut Emerys down before he even had a chance to help. Now he doesn't want anything to do with me." As the sobs began to escape me, Mama tutted and wrapped me in her arms. "We're going to lose everything," I gasped. "And it's all my fault."

"No." Papa rubbed his chin. "The faults with me. I pushed my burdens onto you when I knew *I'd* failed. We'll find a way. I promise you, we will—"

"Why does it sound like you all are giving up?"

I raised my head from Mama's shoulder. Scowling, Drystan threw a piece of cheese at me, and it bounced off my muddy skirts. "You're married to the poor fool. What's he going to do, run away? Pound his door down and make him listen."

Mama threw the cheese back at him and pinged him on the head. "Foul mouth!"

"But I'm right," Drystan continued. "This shouldn't have fallen onto you, Rhia, but it has. If there's anything chance we can save Lians, we have to take it."

I laid against Mama's shoulder, letting their words sink in. *Love is self-sacrifice.* What could I sacrifice to a man who doesn't love me? That I don't love?

But don't you?

With a squeak, a tiny mouse crept from the cupboards, inching his way toward the cheese. Slowly, a smile spread across my face. I may not have something to sacrifice, but I did have something I could give. I kissed Mama's and Papa's cheeks, then Drystan's. The latter groaned and wiped his cheek. "What was that for?"

"For giving me an idea." Grinning, I took the butter knife off the table, spinning as I flicked my wrist. The knife thudded into the floor, spearing the mouse through the back. *Bullseye.*

Drystan yelped. "Stop doing that!"

"Rhia," Mama's skin turned green. "I think you may have some anger issues we need to talk about."

Ignoring them, I wrapped the poor creature in a napkin and stuffed it in my pocket. About time Jacc had some real food—I needed to remind him what home felt like.

And needed to *show* Emerys what a home was in the first place.

15

"A chance."

My lungs burned like the hot peppers Mama grew in the summer by the time I reached the castle. *How many times am I going to run this distance in one story?* This was it—my last chance, and I had to make it count, do it right.

I made a stop into the kitchens, gasping as I thanked the cook on duty. The bloke gave me a confused look as he passed me my requested item, along with a polite wave as I bolted off again. In the main hall, I nearly colliding with Wynny as I barreled toward my suite. Out of the corner of my eye, I saw her grinning in my direction.

Once inside my room, I tossed the still sleeping Jacc his mouse. It spiraled through the air before landing directly onto his front paws. The wretched creature gave the rodent two quick sniffs before hissing his displeasure.

At least someone had taken well to royal life.

Gasping for breath, I pulled the box containing my ruined

wedding dress from under my bed. *Sorry, Mama.* I dumped the torn, stained heap on the floor, shoving the contents from the kitchens into the box, along with a few trinkets I'd grabbed from my hut and on the way back to the castle.

Now that the sun had broken through the clouds, I opened my windows, letting light pour over the roses on the sill. Smiling at them, I grabbed my box and ran out of the room.

Sweat poured down my face and back, my entire body aching, by the time I reached Emerys' suite. *So many bloody stairs.* Sucking in heavy breaths, coughing, I banged on his door, vibrations ringing back into my fist.

Nothing.

My eyes narrowed. *You can't get rid of me that easily.* I knocked again, more gently, forcefully slowing my breathing, adjusting the box propped against my hip.

Nothing. Not even any movement.

I jiggled the doorknob and was surprised to find it unlocked. Turning it, I let the heavy door swing all the way open before I stepped inside. Just like mine, Emerys' suite had two rooms—the outer sitting area, where the bed was located, along with his desk. The inner chamber held the bathing room and closet.

Please, don't be naked. Cringing, I peeked into the inner chamber, breathing out a sigh of relief when I found it empty. Even though he wasn't here, a tall fire still burned in the hearth—courtesy of Catrin, no doubt.

Anxiety clawed at my stomach as I moved deeper inside. I ran my fingers along the edge of his desk, the papers once strewn across it now neatly stacked and tucked into a velum leaflet.

Like I'd noted the night before, Emerys had done nothing to personalize his chambers. Nothing to bring life to his space, nothing to make the room feel like *him.*

I'm not comfortable here, the room screamed. Almost as if he'd only ever planned on staying for a visit.

Had Emerys ever felt comfortable anywhere?

I set my box down on his perfectly made bed and leaned against the frame. If only I could turn back time, start over. Maybe keep turning until I could pluck him from his father's grasp before the torment began.

"Come to insult him more?"

My heart leaped into my throat. I looked up just as Catrin hobbled through the doorway, weathered lips smirking, carrying a basket full of clean laundry.

Before she could fight, I stepped forward and took the laundry from her. "I never meant to insult him."

"Hmm." Was all Catrin said as she followed me into the inner chamber towards the closet. I just needed something to keep my hands busy, something to distract me from her piercing stare— as if she could see all the way through to the black parts of my soul.

She watched, amused, as I repeatedly tried to fold one of Emerys' doublets, but the crease wouldn't stay. After the tenth attempt, I cursed, throwing it back into the basket. With a slight smile, Catrin limped over and picked up the doublet. Folding it slowly enough so I could memorize her technique until it lay in a perfect smooth square. She placed it on one of the shelves in his closet.

Hand over my throat, willing my pulse to slow, I asked. "Why do you still tend to him?"

Catrin artfully folded an undershirt. "I don't see how that's your business?"

I earned that one. I chewed the inside of my cheek. "I'm sure any of the other servants could do this work for you, but you choose to. Why?"

"Does your mother still do your laundry for you?" Catrin arched her wiry brow. "Clean for you? Cook for you?"

I twisted my sweaty, wind-blown hair around my fingers. "Yes—well—she did, until recently."

The way Catrin looked at me had me crawling back into a sensation I hadn't felt in a long time—that of a scolded child. She smiled, licking her lips. "And now someone else does it, I presume?"

I nodded.

"So, it seems that you and Emerys aren't so different, after all?"

That was the first time she'd used his name in front of me. "I never said we were."

"Not out loud." Catrin blew out a sigh. "But you've done a fine job of showing it."

Guilt coiled in my gut, but desperation caused me to push her. "I wish you'd answer my question."

Catrin started on a pair of wool socks. "I raised him. I'm sure that goose, Wynny, told you as much. Even as a freshly born babe, his mother never fed him from her breast."

I couldn't help it—I gagged. "But *you* did?"

"Lord, no." Her watery eyes widened. "Goat's milk, stupid girl, goat's milk!"

I let out a nervous laugh, and Catrin continued. "I taught him his letters and numbers, kissed his skinned knees, cried with him when his heart was broken."

It was challenging to imagine Catrin that vulnerable. Her eyes passed over me, assessing. "So, that is—princess—why I still fold his clothes. Have you ever cared for someone without expecting anything in return?"

"Yes." I steeled myself against her stare. "For Lians . . . and Jacc."

"Who, may I ask, is Jacc?"

"My cat." Catrin's brows furrowed in confusion, so I clarified, shrugging. "He's old and fat. I hunt for him."

Catrin burst into a haughty laugh—making me jump—then said. "Why are you here, little guppy?"

That sounded almost endearing. I sighed and slumped onto the floor, taking another doublet from the basket, attempting to mimic her folds. "I don't know, really." As my throat began to tighten, the words started pouring out. "To start over, I think? Since Papa read me the letter from the King, announcing the matching—*not asking*—I've been so afraid of being forced into becoming someone I'm not. I never stopped to think that maybe Lians needed someone better than me to save it," I exhaled. "That they needed Princess Rhiannon . . . and not just Rhia."

Catrin just nodded, continuing her folding on the laundry table. "How astute of you."

My brows pinched. "What?"

"Insightful."

"Are you mocking me?"

"Of course, I am," Catrin chuckled. "But that doesn't diminish your . . . astuteness."

"Thank you." I pursed my lips. "I guess."

Catrin folded the last piece of clothing and placed it gently on her neat stack. I gave her what I'd done to add to the pile. She sniffed loudly. "And how, exactly, Princess Rhiannon, do you plan to remedy this situation?"

I have to do this. For Lians. For Papa. I have to do this. The image of Wynny's note flashed through my mind, and I shook my head. "I—" I gulped. "I am going to apologize."

"Apology accepted."

I yelped, leaping off the floor. Catrin let out a snorting laugh.

Emerys stood in the doorway of the inner chamber, arms crossed but expression soft.

How long had he been standing there? I glared at her at Catrin and she winked at me. *Old hag.* She bent over to pick the empty laundry basket off the floor, then shuffled for the door, patting Emerys' shoulder as she passed. "Call if you need anything."

"Thank you." Emerys nodded to her, but his eyes were fixed on me.

This room's too small. Cheeks burning, I sidled past him to the sitting room. The box I laid on his bed didn't look disturbed. Thank goodness. At least he wasn't nosy.

Once Catrin had waddled out of the suite, closing the door behind her, I cleared my throat, tucking my filthy skirts beneath me as I sat on his sofa. The hand on the clock clicked noisily as we stared each other down.

It annoyed me how much I'd missed his face. Not just for his lovely features, but the little quirks and emotions behind them. His lips twitched to the side as he chewed his bottom lip, uncertain. "Though, it would help to know what you're apologizing for."

I stared down at my hands, rubbing my wrists. "You know what about."

His lips curled. "You mistake me—I'd like to *hear* you say it."

I shot him a glare, then exhaled. *I earned that one, too.* "Fine— I've been . . . unpleasant."

Emerys' smile widened. "You have been unpleasant, haven't you?"

"Don't push me," I growled back.

Emerys shoved his hands in his pockets, staring into the fire as he moved to the hearth. "I'll be the one in question if I don't confess that I owe *you* an apology, as well. I should have never spoken so sharply yesterday. I'm sorry."

"Don't worry about it." I leaned back, settling into the cushions. "It's been a stressful month—for both of us."

Emerys nodded, though I didn't miss the sadness hovering over him.

I remembered the box on the bed and a thrill ran through me. Smiling, I caught Emerys' eye, holding it despite the uncertainty I saw there. "I want you to play along with me, all right?" I took a shaky breath. "And don't think I'm doing this because of what you've told me about the King. Nice words won't make a difference in that regard, so stop looking so nervous."

Emerys nodded again, watching me warily.

I reached out my hand and breathed a sigh of relief when he took it. Guiding, I sat him on the sofa where I'd been, then scooted the tea table in front of him.

He raised a brow. I raised my finger and smiled. "Close your eyes."

He did.

I lifted the box from the bed and placed it on the tea table. "Open them," I said, stretching my arms wide.

Emerys blinked at the box, confused, then blinked up at me. "What is it?"

"Ta-da!" Heat crept across my chest and neck. "It's an apology box."

Recognition flashed across his features. *This must be normal in the courts.* Emerys reached for the box, but I stopped him, grinning. "Slowly, please. This one is special."

"Oh?" He said, but the twinkle in his eyes made the thrill in my stomach so much stronger.

I nodded. "Not only is it an apology—it's a gift."

Emerys frowned. "Is it a snail? If so, you can have it back."

"No," I snapped, and he smiled. "It's what you've always wanted."

His eyes narrowed into slits. Scooting to the edge of the sofa, he slid the lid off the box. The first thing he lifted from it was a crusty, brown loaf of bread. Brows raised, he peered up at me, questioning.

I tucked my hands behind my back. "My favorite smell in the entire world is fresh bread, still hot from the oven."

Still skeptical, he next took out a dried, pressed daffodil. He turned it gently over his palm, studying it. "You're favorite flower." Emerys smiled slowly, catching on. "And color?"

I nodded. "Like the sun."

His next smile nearly crumpled my heart. "And like the

roses? They said I should have gone with red, but it didn't feel right."

Somehow, he knew. I nodded again. "Yes, like the roses, too."

Next, he lifted the small doll Mama had knitted me as a child —an orange kitten, a perfect replica of Jacc when he was small.

"Your favorite animal," he said, not a question.

I took the doll from him and pressed it under my chin. "If you ever hurt my cat, I'll kill you."

"I wouldn't dream of it," Emerys said. "Only monsters hurt animals for anything other than food . . . unless they're snails. They can just die."

"See?" I batted my lashes the way Wynny showed me. "Your gift is helping already."

Emerys picked up the daffodil again, pressing it gently between his fingers. "My gift is a chance, isn't it?"

"Yes."

After a pause, Emerys leapt to his feet, holding his arm out for me. "I'll take it. Care for a stroll, my lady?"

Inhaling, my focus zeroed in on his extended elbow. *Lians . . . I can do this for Lians.*

But maybe . . . just maybe, I could do this for me, too.

Keeping my back as straight as possible, I gave Emerys my best curtsy before accepting his arm. "Entertain me, prince. Let's see what you're capable of."

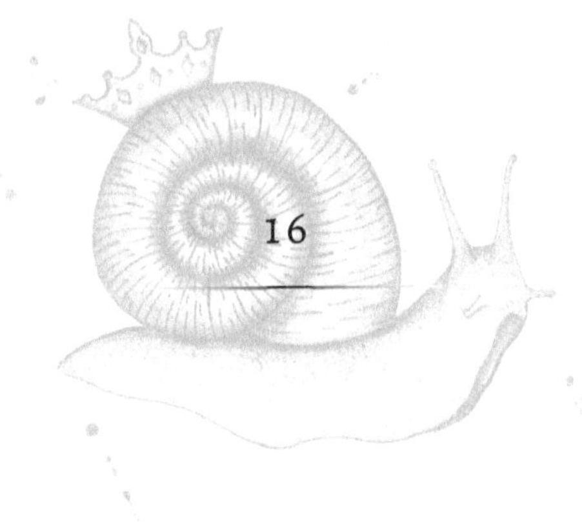

16

"A painting most lovely."

I wasn't as uncomfortable as I expected, walking arm and arm with him.

Emerys kept his touch light, barely brushing the fabric of my sleeve. The silence as we descended into the south courtyard easy instead of awkward. He didn't press me to talk, unlike everyone else, and I didn't push him. Emerys seemed content to watch the sky, tripping more than once on his own feet.

Unlike the central courtyard, inside the portcullis, the south yard was overgrown with wildflowers instead of thorns. They grew between the cracks in the cobblestone, in every open patch of green. Bluebells grew along the far stone wall, encircling a rickety bench and shaded by a large blooming magnolia tree. As we sat, I closed my eyes and exhaled, so grateful for the sun tickling my face. When I opened them again, I found Emerys' attention still on the sky, a slight smile dancing on his lips.

I watched him for a while before finally asking. "What are you looking at?"

A blush rose beneath his fair skin. "The birds. I—I love them. Always have. We don't have blackcaps and cuckoos out west like you do here."

"I've lived here my entire life," I pondered. "And I have no idea what blackcaps or cuckoos are."

Emerys pointed to a thin branch above us—to where a small grey bird with a black, feather bowl on its head sat.

"Ah," I said. "Blackcaps, I get it."

"Beautiful, aren't they?" Emerys beamed. "They like to gorge themselves on the bilberries. I could watch them all day."

I glanced around. Besides the flowers and a run-down well at the center, the courtyard sat empty. A vision of bonfires and fairy lights filled my mind, the summer parties we could have, of painted birdhouses filled with seeds so that everyone could enjoy the blackcaps and cuckoos. I smiled at him. "You should build a sanctuary for them."

Emerys brightened. "How wonderful would that be—" He hesitated.

"What?" I asked.

He chewed his lip. "I'm waiting for the part where you laugh at me."

"Why would I laugh?"

Emerys leaned back, stretching his long legs and shrugged. "It's not very princely to enjoy birdsong more than swordplay. You wouldn't be the first to laugh."

Tormented for being a peaceful person—that's the world we lived in. Criticized for enjoying the little things. "Well, there are worse things to love," I said.

"Such as?"

I crinkled my nose. "Mutton."

Emerys laughed. "No roasted lamb's leg for you?"

I made a gagging gesture, and he laughed again. Such a soft, sweet sound. "I'll remember that."

The way his eyes passed over my face, lingering on my lips, made my stomach twist. I stood, breathless. "Have you seen the creek?"

"I haven't had the pleasure," Emerys replied.

I took his elbow and led him from the courtyard out into the fields behind the castle. Trudging through knee-high grass, it was about a mile walk to the edge of the forest, where the creek separated Lians' boundaries from the Wentwood. As we walked, I caught Emerys watching me.

I shot him a glare. "What?"

He jerked away so fast he tripped, nearly face planting into the reeds. He straightened, brushing off his trousers, and cleared his throat. "It's nothing."

"Liar," I said, still laughing from the nosedive. "Tell me what you're thinking."

Panic flickered over Emerys' features. "It's just—oh, look!" He pointed at something ahead of me. I looked, and he gestured again to a black and white bird with a pointy feather on the back of its head, sitting in a bush. "That's called a lapwing," he said. "They prefer open terrain and marshland. Did you know that over seventy percent of Gwent is wooded?"

"I'm aware," I snorted.

He nodded, and I decided to let the previous subject drop . . . for now.

When we reached the edge of the creek, the sun had moved to mid-day, the intensity of its rays blinding as it reflected off the surface of the gently moving water. Boughs from the forest trees stretched over the creek, providing shade. I made to sit on a boulder along the waterline, but Emerys stopped me, laying his cloak over the stone before gesturing with a smile for me to sit.

My first instinct was to snap back, to tell him I wasn't afraid to get wet, but I held my tongue. *Be nice, Rhia.* Instead, I rolled my eyes before making a show of getting comfortable atop his cloak. His brows rose, amused, and I gave him a coy smile.

Emerys yanked off his boots, rolling up his pant legs, and waded into the calf-deep water. Bending down, he picked through the array of stones lining the creek bed, those large eyes holding such childlike joy. It was hard to imagine the coldness I'd seen that first night we'd met, that I'd seen even just yesterday. *I wonder if he thinks the same about me.*

I picked a bit of moss off the boulder, tearing it up between my fingers. "So, you're a rock collector, too?"

Inspecting a shiny green stone, he said. "It's not uncommon for a person to have more than one interest."

I shrugged. "I suppose not."

"And you?" He glanced up at me, dark hair falling in his eyes. "What are your interests?"

"Me?"

"Do you see anyone else here?"

I slumped forward, resting my elbows on my thighs. *What* do *I like to do?* I thought back to my childhood, to days spent running free in the fields—until they passed my death sentence —marriage. What had I ever done besides work? Even as a toddler, I collected eggs and helped carry grain to the livestock.

It took me longer than I'd have liked to answer. Emerys watched me intently. "I like to walk. Through the woods, over to the next village, if I can. Anywhere as long as I can explore."

"And the woods are your favorite." Again, not a question.

I nodded.

"And you can't take those walks anymore because of the Wildmen."

I nodded again, slower, stiffer—angrier. "They've always been a threat, but it wasn't so bad until the last couple years. I had more freedom, then."

Instead of pushing further, Emerys nodded and returned to his rocks, head snapping up occasionally at the chirp of a nearby bird. Not a killer. Not a politician. But peaceful.

Curiosity struck me. "Did you ever learn to use a sword?"

"I did." Emerys washed a bit of mud off a round pink stone. "And a spear, bow, and axe."

He passed the stone to me, and I cupped it in my palm. It was pretty—almost translucent, seeming to glow in the light. "Were you good at it?"

Emerys chuckled. "I'm decent, but I doubt I'd be any good in real warfare. There are many types of men in the world, and not all of them are suited for combat. I flinch too much."

"Fair enough." I tucked the stone in my pocket. "Most men aren't that honest, either, in my experience."

Emerys gave me a crooked smile. "And you have . . . lots of experience?"

Arrogant trout. I glared. "Shove it."

He burst out laughing as heat crept up my neck. Terrorizing more moss, I couldn't stop myself from asking. "What about you? Do you have . . . experience?"

It was his turn to redden as he returned quickly to picking at stones. "Er, um, no."

I chomped down on the inside of my cheek to keep from grinning. "Any at all?"

Poor Emerys turned as tomato red as he had on our wedding night. "Ah, no. None."

"Me, either," I exhaled, cupping my chin. "How unlucky for the both of us."

"I think we're quite lucky, to be honest."

"Really?"

When he looked at me this time, it was with a full-blown grin. "Yes. I'm glad to know you don't have any unfortunate diseases that would be of concern to my health."

"Ha." My lips curled into a cruel smile. "It's your people with warts. A poor man's disease is a bad back and dirt-stained hands." I paused, letting our laughter die. The following words escaped before I could stop them. "Why did you come here? Agree to marry me?"

The smile in Emerys' eyes faded, and he sucked in a sharp breath, turning his new treasures over in his palms. "Please, don't be offended, but I didn't."

"How dare you!" I gasped—but when he looked up, panicked—I smiled, waving him off. "I'm kidding, relax. Please, continue."

Emerys swallowed, throat bobbing. "My father is not a . . . gracious ruler, as I'm sure you're aware. He keeps the kingdom running, in line, but his needs always come first. A man could be dying of knife wound in front of him, and he'd horde the bandages away with the excuse he may need them for himself later." He exhaled, cheeks pink from the sun. "About half a year back, I told him as such—questioned his caring for those below him, for lack of a better word."

I kept still, silent, afraid of scaring him away like one the birds he loved so well.

Emerys sat on the bank beside me, inspecting his new stones. "A few months later, I received a letter from a rural messenger—my marriage alliance to the region of Gwent had been accepted. Punishment for speaking out against him, I figured. What bothered me most was that my father didn't have the balls to tell me himself. He let a courier do it."

"I'm sorry," I whispered. *The old hag was right. He and I aren't so different.*

"Don't apologize." Emerys chewed his thumbnail. "In fact, I should be apologizing to you . . . again. Everything that's happened is my fault. I confronted him again after getting the message. He said that Gwent is a doomed country. If I saw myself as some high and mighty ruler, then he'd make me one. Plus, he'd found me a bride worthy of my station."

A peasant girl for a sixth son who would never inherit a kingdom.

Emerys tossed a rock into the creek with a loud plunk. "But he never meant for me to succeed in saving Lians. I realize that now. It was all just another one of his games. I thought I could make him proud, change his mind about me. He'd probably arranged the invading host as soon as I'd left. All he wanted was to humiliate me, teach me a lesson. Appearances are everything to him, and now he could ruin mine."

"But we can still save it." I slid off the rock to sit beside him. "I finished your drainage plans. We could start growing crops again." My words came too fast, way too fast. "Papa wants to start draining the rest of the fields. He even agreed to pull down the old storage building so we can use the stone. If the King could give us an extension on our debt, we can repair the village. We can start selling again. We can—"

"By the end of the week?" Emerys interrupted. "The King wants money, not progress. As I said, he'd made up his mind about Lians a long time ago."

"So, we do nothing?" I grabbed his hand and squeezed— hard. "We give up?"

Emerys looked away, sadness passing over his face. A sparrow flew past, soaring toward the castle—our castle—on the hilltop. After a moment, he turned to me, hesitant. "Have you ever seen the sea?"

I blinked, taken aback. "N-no, but what does that have to do with anything—"

"Let's leave." His smile was brighter than any ray of sun that'd touched my skin. "We could go to the ocean. Maybe find a ship and sail. Explore, see the world." He squeezed my hand back, making my heart leap. "Be free."

The pieces slowly clicked into place. "No wonder you like those birds so well. It's because they can fly away, isn't it? Freedom."

"We don't have to stay here, Rhia," Emerys said.

He'd never called me just Rhia before.

Even still, I leaned back. "And we just leave everyone to the wolves once your father cleans them out? Leave my family?"

"Not for forever," He mused. "We can make sure they've settled somewhere new first." Emerys leaned forward, and my body went rigid as he gently ran his fingers through a strand of my hair. "When have we ever done something for ourselves? Either of us? Just lived?"

Oh, what a beautiful picture he painted, and I could see it. The vibrant sails of our very own ship whipping in the breeze. Salty ocean air kissing my wind-burnt face. We could fly away somewhere warm, where the sun always shone.

Together—friends, and maybe even more than that.

He folded my hands in his, and I relished the smoothness of his skin, the absolute absurdity of it. Not calloused, not rough or angry, but gentle. Kind.

Deserving.

I could leave. Start fresh.

I almost said as such, but my mind flashed to my mother—shaving Papa's furry leg in our shamble of a home. Where the roof leaked, where ice formed inside the windows on winter nights. Where I spent countless days hoping I made it to the next, imagining what my next meal would taste like.

Who would stand for them?

Yes, it was a beautiful picture he painted—and one that could never be.

Reluctantly, I slid my fingers from his and cupped his cheek. Emerys closed his eyes, leaning into my hand. *Is he so starved for a caring touch?* I whispered, "We can't leave."

His eyes fluttered open, locking onto mine. "Why not?"

"Because love is sacrifice." I let out a long sigh. "And I love my people, and I will fight for them until my dying breath. No matter what I truly want."

I thought he'd pull away, but Emerys pressed his cheek deeper into my palm. "You can't save them, Rhia."

I smiled. "Watch me."

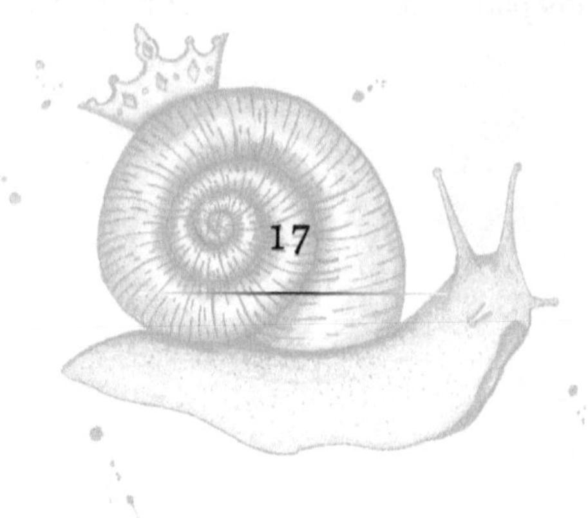

17

"Pity party crashers."

"I can't do that." Emerys sat back, face sinking. "My father's host will be here any day. *You can't save Lians.*"

I leaned into him, stopping his retreat. "We can still fight. We can—"

"We can what?" Emerys asked. "Fight them off?" He gestured toward the village. "There's maybe . . . thirty men strong enough to fight? Are you suggesting that the elderly, women, and children beat away trained soldiers with brooms and cooking spoons?"

"No, I—" *Well, he has me there.* I jutted my chin. "I'll fight them."

"With your fists?" Emerys snorted. "You said the Wildmen stole all the weapons."

"I'll tenderize them with a rock if I have to." I cocked my head, remembering. "Or I can use that pretty hammer you sent Caddic."

134

Emerys' brows knit together. "Hammer?"

"You didn't send Caddic a hammer?"

"I have no idea what you're talking about."

Huh. Interesting. A question for later. I dropped the subject. "Never mind."

Emerys shook his head, chuckling. "If even a third of the court had your spirit, Wales would be unstoppable."

"Then let's be unstoppable." I grasped his shoulders. "I know there's a way."

Gently, he placed his hands over mine. "You won't leave with me?"

I held his gaze, unwavering. "No."

Without blinking, in the same breath, he asked, "Do you love me?"

My stomach dropped, hitting my lower intestines, then bouncing back into my throat. "How could you ask that? I barely know you."

"I love you," Emerys whispered, eyes falling, and my world fell into a spiral with them. "You're strong. Confident. Everything I always wanted to be. I knew that when I first saw you in that horrifying wedding gown—a soldier heading to war."

I could barely breathe over the lump in my throat. "Only on the outside. You wouldn't like what you'd see if you looked inside." Hateful, angry, vindictive. Could I have done what Emerys had? Stand up to Papa and face the consequences so gracefully? Sure, I'd given Papa more than one nasty comment but never pushed back. Not when he put Lians at risk with his decisions, not when he'd announced that I'd be the one paying for those choices.

Emerys stroked my cheek. "But you'll never love me, will you? Because I *am* the enemy."

I choked. *More time, I just need more time.*

He set my hands gently into my lap then stood, turning away from the creek—from me.

Despite the shocked numbness still invading my limbs, I grabbed his sleeve. "You can't just say things like that, then walk away. Where are you going?"

He pulled away, glancing over his shoulder. "I'm going home."

No, no, no. I swallowed, eyes burning. "To the castle?"

"To Aberaron." He shook his head. "I won't be dragged back to court like a fool. Let me have some dignity."

"Who cares what he thinks? What anyone thinks?" *No, no, no, no.* He couldn't leave me now. "You're going to let him keep bullying you?"

"I'm used to being stomped on. Nothing will be new."

And just like that, he walked away—the hope that'd unknowingly grown in my heart going up in smoke.

"Coward," I hissed through clenched teeth.

Emerys froze in his tracks.

My hands curled into fists, nails biting into my palms. "I convinced myself that you couldn't be the royal devil that I'd expected. I gave you the chance to prove me wrong, but you're something worse, aren't you? A frail, yellow-bellied coward."

I hated myself for saying it as soon as the words passed my lips. The cold mask he wore when we met locked over Emerys' features. I would never let him know how badly it hurt to see that face again.

Not as he opened his mouth to respond. Not as his eyes passed over my shoulder and grew wide, his body going rigid.

Terror rolled through every vein, pushing adrenaline into my blood. I wheeled.

A Wildman stood just on the other side of the creek. I knew him instantly—the young man that kneed Emerys in the groin. Still dressed in deerskin, a large axe propped over his shoulder, his black eyes glinted in recognition as he glanced between the prince and me.

He grinned, front teeth browned with rot. "And here I

thought the squirrel I ate this morning would be the best part of my day." He stepped forward into the water as I backed away. I dared look over my shoulder to Emerys. He reached for me, but he would never close the distance between us in time. I knew the look in the Wildman's gaze—violence.

I caught Emerys eye, letting the emotions I saw there sink into my bones—fear . . . for me. Not for himself, not for Lians. Not from his father's host coming for us—just me.

It gave me strength, a calm clearness seeping through my mind. I smiled at Emerys—at my husband—and whispered, "Run."

———

I'd like to say I had a clever quip ready to describe this moment, but adrenaline shot my wit straight out my earholes like hot butter, letting my survival instincts kick in.

Hearing my order, the Wildman burst into a sprint, tearing through the creek, water spraying over his long, stringy hair.

I grabbed Emerys' hand as I bolted past him, dragging him along behind. He caught his steps, catching up. Before I knew it, Emerys rushed ahead, the two of us barreling toward the castle. The Wildman's heavy boots behind us pounded like thunder, his heavy breaths tar dripping down my skin.

The tall grass whipped against my arms and legs, burning like a thousand bee stings. Emerys tripped, but I didn't slow, dragging him along behind like a rider with his foot caught in his stirrup.

The Wildman's laugh rippled through me, and I yanked Emerys so hard my shoulder popped, pain shooting through me, but he caught his footing. I dared a look back—the man hot on our tail—and a thought struck me.

I veered off course, heading toward the village. Emerys

pulled against my grip, but I overpowered him. "This way!" I called.

Skin flushed with exertion, he called back. "Where are we going?"

I tried to respond, but my voice was drowned out by the Wildman's. "You're only delaying your coming beating, kiddos! Might as well give up now!"

I shot him a rude gesture with my free hand, never slowing. Despite everything, Emerys laughed.

We needed to shake him but leading him into the castle would be chaos. Too many unprepared, pampered city folk that didn't know how to throw a proper punch. They'd be massacred. Whether he meant to kill us, kidnap us, or just beat us to an inch of our lives, as he'd implied, the village was our best hope now.

I kept off the road, hoping to slow our pursuer, but he hadn't given any indication of wearing down. My lungs were on fire, muscles in my thighs beginning to numb. I couldn't imagine how Emerys must be fairing. The thought only pushed me harder.

As the hillcrest fell, revealing Lians below, I tightened my grip on Emerys, steering us toward the mudflats that sat below a second rise.

Emerys' breaths were coming in gasps. He couldn't keep this pace much longer. I cried out in relief as we passed over the next hill, dodging to the left—sending the Wildman tumbling straight into my newly dug retention pond. He screamed as he fell, but I didn't allow us to slow. Not yet—not until we'd skirted the outside of the flats, into the forest behind.

"Here." Emerys pulled down behind a rotten log. I skid, damp earth clinging to my skin, wet with sweat. I pressed myself into the log, the heavy scent of moss and decomposing wood filling my nose. I nearly shot out of my skin as Emerys' arms wrapped around my torso. It took a moment for me to realize that it was a hug.

"Are you alright?" He whispered through gasping breaths, dark hair sticking to the sweat dripping down his temples. I pushed back, hands against his chest, and a jolt of pain shot through my shoulder. I winced, clutching it. "I'm an arm down, but fine. You?"

"Fine." Emerys peered over the log towards the open flats, breaths finally slowing. "How long before he gets out of there?

"Unless he broke his leg, he already has." I straightened, limbs trembling.

"Do you think he's still after us?"

"Of course he is," I answered. "He wants something, and I doubt it's just to give us a beating."

Emerys nodded. "Most likely to ransom us." He rose to a crouch, taking in the forest. "Come on. We need to alert the village."

I grabbed his arm. "No."

Emerys raised his brows in surprise.

"If we raise the alarm, he *will* run," I said, stern. "But if we can capture him, we can get answers."

"You want to capture him? Have you lost your mind?" Emerys shook his head. "Did you not see the *giant* axe he's carrying?"

"Exactly. It's Caddic's," I shot back. "I bet he'd like it back. We need to find out where they're holed up."

I thought he'd continue to argue, but instead, Emerys smiled. "There's no way I'll be able to change your mind, is there?"

I smiled back, climbing to my feet. "Not a chance. Follow me, princeling."

We crept from our hiding place. Around us, the forest was silent—a clear indication the Wildman still lingered in the area. I gestured for Emerys to keep close. Body low, footsteps light, I moved to the tree line. I peeked around a tree trunk, scanning—

no sign of our unexpected guest. He probably assumed we'd headed into the village. Now, he's staying hidden, waiting for us to expose ourselves.

A loud crack sounded behind me, and I nearly leaped out of my skin as I whirled. Emerys looked up at me, eyes wide, a broken twig beneath his foot.

"Snap another one, and I'll snap your neck," I hissed, clutching my pounding heart.

He pursed his lips, but his next step was softer. "Excuse me, your highness. Not all of us are skilled in the art of stalking around like a criminal."

I stuck out my tongue, and he chuckled under his breath. *Why do I love that laugh so much?* I shook the thought away, moving forward. After several yards in complete silence, I couldn't control the urge to glance back. Behind me, Emerys smiled. My brows rose in question.

"What were you thinking about?" he asked with that cheeky smile.

"What do you mean?"

Emerys shook his head rapidly, mimicking me. Heat burned up my neck, and he grinned. "Was it about me?"

I turned away, the warmth spreading into my cheeks. "Go away."

"Never."

The word made my stomach clench. Again, I looked back. This time, Emerys blushed, and he cleared his throat. "How could I? This is the most fun I've had in years."

Never. He wouldn't leave. I hoped he couldn't see the overflowing of emotion pouring out of my calming heart. I grinned back. "You really are insane, aren't you?"

"Perhaps so."

We hovered on the edge of the forest behind Mama and Papa's hut. From here, I could see Drystan's snail house. Besides the chickens pecking around the yard, no one seemed to be home—thank God.

Emerys stepped up beside me. "What's your plan?"

I bit my lip. *A plan would have been a good idea.* I spit out the first thing that came to mind. "Get inside and find anything possible we can use as a weapon."

Emerys swallowed. "Do you think he's watching for us?"

"Definitely." *Predators don't give up the hunt that easily.*

Emerys' attention snapped to our right, deeper into the forest. My body stilled as I strained to listen over the blood pounding in my ears.

"There." Emerys nodded toward trees. "Did you hear that?"

I held my breath. Nothing. I shook my head.

Emerys eyes shifted back and forth as if hoping to see through the shadows cast by the canopy. He jumped. "There it is again."

I took his hand and squeezed. "What does it sound like?"

"Moaning?" Emerys furrowed his brow. "Someone's out there. Maybe he's injured."

"Well." I reached down and picked up a fallen branch, about as thick as my wrist. "No one lives forever, right? Let's go."

Emerys placed his fist over his heart in salute, grabbing a nearby branch, as well.

Sucking in a few deep breaths, I turned and pushed my way through the brush. Cringing with every step, with every bit of undergrowth snagging on my skirts. *The one day I decided not to wear pants.* Emerys followed my steps exactly, hand over his mouth in an attempt to quiet his breathing.

The wind carried a low moan through the trees.

There. Three yards ahead. Maybe the Wildman had broken something after all. I raised my branch, inhaling, and signaled to Emerys where I'd heard the noise. He nodded, staying low.

Another moan.

Sucking in another breath, I lunged. Wailing like a

maddened bull as I charged through the brush—only to find my brother and Wynny in various stages of undress.

They screamed.

I screamed.

Emerys shielded his eyes as Wynny frantically yanked her bodice back into place, dark curls free down to her waist, skirts shoved up to compromising heights.

"Lord above—" Drystan scrambled with his trouser laces. "Why are you trying to kill us?"

"I wasn't trying to kill *you*!" I groaned, "I was *going* to kill a Wildman."

Behind me, Emerys still covered his eyes. I threw my branch at him. "It's safe now, you maiden."

Emerys peeked through his fingers, then fixed his gaze far from his cousin—whose cheeks were on fire. "We were attacked by the creek. We heard you and thought . . . er . . . you were him."

Wynny groaned, hiding behind her hands. Drystan gave her shoulder a loving pat, not embarrassed in the slightest. He gestured to the branch Emerys clutched. "And you thought you'd take him out with that?" His green eyes widened. "Mama, Papa—"

"They're not at the house," I said. "We lost the Wildman at the flats. For now. We're going to lure him out and capture him."

Drystan glanced between Emerys and me, back and forth, until they finally settled on the prince. "Are you stupid? Wait—I take that back. Of course, you are. Only you would come up with a plan like that."

Emerys bristled. "Says the man who barreled after four of them, screaming like an imbecile."

"At least I wasn't toting my woman along."

"Excuse me?" I growled.

"She's scarier than you, trust me," Emerys continued. "And speaking of which—"

As he and Drystan flew into an argument, I caught Wynny smiling at me.

"*What?*" I mouthed. She flicked her chin toward Emerys.

"*Did you use my suggestion?*" She mouthed back.

I rolled my eyes. "*Yes, I made an apology box, you delinquent.*"

Wynny giggled behind her hand just as Emerys grabbed my hand. "Come on." I could almost imagine smoke pouring out his nostrils. He shot Drystan a venomous glare. "I'm done with him. We're running out of time. We need to find that filthy, piece of garbage—"

"Find who now?"

My heart stopped.

The four of us wheeled. Behind us, the Wildman grinned, grasping his axe with both hands. "No, please, don't stop for me. Finish your thought, boy."

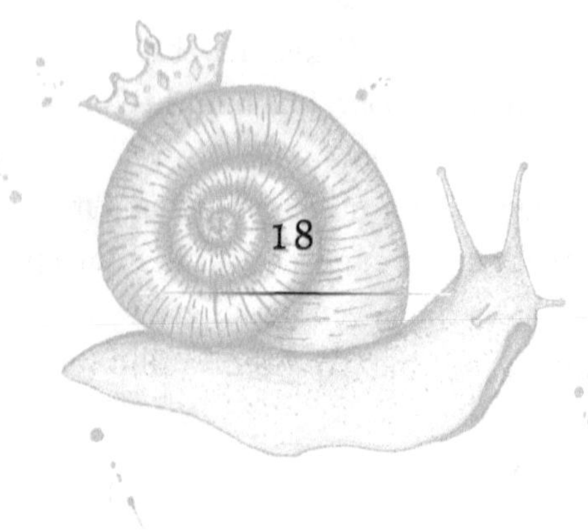

18

"Watch for the lion ahead."

N eedless to say—we bolted.

The four of us sprinted out of the forest at top speed, not daring to look back. Fortunately, the Wildman's newly acquired limp slowed him. It didn't take long for us to reach my family's yard. Squawking, wings flapping, the chickens scattered, flying up into our faces.

Wynny tripped, crying out as her knees hit the rocky ground. Drystan scooped her out of the dirt and managed to keep running.

"Get her out of here." I cried to him, and my brother nodded. He and Wynny vanished behind the hut, toward the horse pastures.

Protect her. Drystan would ride them to the castle. There was no one I trusted more with my only friend's safety. I glanced over my shoulder. The Wildman was nearly across the field. He'd be on us in seconds.

"In here." I grabbed Emerys' hand and drug him into my parent's hut, cursing as I banged my injured shoulder on the edge of the door. Once on the inside, Emerys pressed his back against the wall, breathing heavily. "Whatever you're going to do, do it fast."

"I'm going. I'm going." I tore through Mama's cabinets, looking for something—anything—with the potential for murder. "You know, if you have any ideas, I'm wearing my listening ears."

"Funny." Emerys leaned over to peer out the window. "If it pleases you, I'm currently trying to recall my fisticuffs lessons."

I paused. "Fisticuffs?"

"You know, hand-to-hand combat."

"I know what it is, idiot."

"Then why did you ask?"

Finally. I wrapped my fingers around the handle of Mama's cook pan. I pointed it at him. "Because I've never heard anyone use that word in serious conversation, that's why."

Emerys grinned. "Please, don't be intimidated by my extraordinary vocabulary."

"Shut up." I crawled to join him by the door. "I've got what I came for. Let's put this joker out of business."

Nose crinkling, Emerys' gaze shifted between me and my makeshift weapon. "A frying pan, really?"

I clutched it against my chest. "Is that a problem?"

"Don't you think that's a little . . ." He shook his head before I could answer. "Nevermind."

Scowling, I pushed him out of the way so I could look out the window myself. From here, the yard appeared empty. The chickens were still on edge, the rooster *bu-gawking* like a hen was about to lay an egg.

I slid back down beside the prince. "Okay, here's the plan," I whispered. Emerys leaned in closer than he needed to listen, his face mere inches from mine. It sent a thrill through me. "He's waiting for us to make the first move. We're not going to give it to him. We'll wait in here until he loses all patience and charges in. That's when I'll attack."

Emerys huffed. "He's not stupid enough to walk in here."

"Of course he is."

"He won't do it."

"Of course he will."

A raspy voice rolled in from outside. "I really wouldn't."

Reflexively, I swung—frying pan connecting with the Wildman's face, peering through the window.

The Wildman doubled over, clutching his face, spewing off a loud stream of curses.

Faster than I could have thought possible, Emerys dove out the window after him. When I got out the door, Emerys had the man pinned to the ground, landing blow after blow to the Wildman's face. "That's for threatening my wife!" Another punch. "That's for my testicles!"

"Stop!" I grabbed Emerys' collar and yanked him off. "He needs to be alive to question him."

The Wildman sat up, coughing as he spat blood. "You think I'm gonna talk? Is that it?"

"You mistake me," I smirked. "I know you will."

"Is that so?" He rose to his knees. "You'd be mistaken, kid, and you probably also made a poor guess in assumin' I came alone, eh?"

My stomach dropped into my bowels. *Oh no.*

Loud, crunching footsteps approached from behind, and Emerys froze. The Wildman smiled, revealing a missing front tooth.

No wonder he'd taken so long to find us—he'd been stalling, waiting for backups to arrive. I wheeled, reaching for Emerys so we could run, but something hard collided with my skull.

My cheek hit the dirt. Emerys cried out. Feet scuffled beside my head. The world went dark.

When my eyes fluttered open, it was not my vision but the sky that was growing dark. I tried to sit up, but a deep aching pain lanced through my temple.

"Easy." A familiar voice whispered. Drystan gripped my arm and helped me sit up, patting my back as I leaned over and vomited. He offered me a drink from his waterskin, and I accepted it gratefully. Taking a sip, I swished it around my mouth then spit it into the dirt. "There's more than one."

Drystan nodded solemnly. "Yeah, I know. We ran into them."

I realized then sweat and grime coated his face. My throat tightened. "Wynny?"

"She's fine." Drystan pulled me to my feet. "As are Mama and Papa."

I wobbled, grabbing his shoulder to steady me. "That's good."

"Rhia?"

My mind was so foggy. I forced myself to look at Drystan's face, to focus, and nearly vomited again at the despair I witnessed there. I croaked. "Yes?"

Drystan swallowed. "Where's the prince?"

19

"Proteges in odd places."

R uins.

Not only had they come for us . . . they'd come to destroy.

Smoke sat over the village in a haze, mingling with the mist and low-hanging clouds. The blacksmith's shop no longer had a roof. They'd ransacked most of the huts. Wails of angered and frightened villagers echoed through the streets.

Standing in the center of the village, my head throbbed as I tried to focus on the voices shouting to me. Seeking guidance, comfort, answers.

I'm so tired. If only they realized I had nothing to give them. I didn't have anything left for myself. But one thing I did know—this attack was done in anger.

And as much as that deep-seated part of me wanted to hate, the new voice growing in my soul understood. Lians has suffered, the Wildmen suffered—but we'd always suffered together. Though we were enemies, our two people always shared common ground—and Emerys destroyed that balance.

Just like my people resented the wealth and indulgence of the nobility, we'd become that to outsiders. With the lights of the wedding feast, the scent of foods richer than they'd ever taste wafting on the breeze—how couldn't they be bitter? But even all these new emotions couldn't lessen my anger for what they'd taken from me—my husband.

That split in my heart continued to crack. We searched everywhere—covered every square inch of the forest, and nothing.

He was just . . . gone.

Vanished. No tracks. No signs of struggle. For the Wildmen, that was nothing new. Papa had sent countless search parties to hunt them down in the past, and nothing ever came of it. How could an entire people leave no trace of their existence? Drystan could learn a thing or two from them. When he left the kitchen, it looked like a windstorm had passed through.

A single tear rolled down my cheek, and I brushed it away, determined not to let anymore fall.

Emerys said he loved me. *Stupid fool.*

After all I'd done to him. Despite how I'd treated him, he'd seen someone worth loving—even when I hadn't been willing to give myself the same courtesy.

And now he was gone, my village in shambles. Worse still, the King's men would be upon us any day—and when they did, I'd have nothing left. I should have listened to Emerys. At least if I'd gone to the sea, we'd still be together.

Despite my best attempts, another tear rolled.

Blocking out the commotion around me, I turned and started the long walk back to the castle, every step a struggle to keep upright as my legs dragged. All the crying and banging made me cringe as people pulled what remained usable out of their homes.

As I passed, they gave me respectful nods, but I saw straight through to the sadness that coated their hearts. I failed them—in more ways than they'd ever know.

By the time I entered the main courtyard, the burst blisters on my heels had filled my boots with blood. Beside the stairwell leading into the grand entry, Drystan held Wynny in his arms, her face pressed into his shoulder.

When they heard me approaching, they turned, but he didn't let her go. Tears stained Wynny's red-rimmed eyes—her cousin was gone, and I hadn't protected him. As I moved toward the stairwell, she stepped towards me, reaching out—and I hurried past them.

If I had to listen to one more apology, one more word of encouragement, I'd snap. More than that, I couldn't bear the guilt. Silence—that's what I needed.

The servants gave me a wide berth as I passed through the halls. Their faces held no pity—they were angry and had every right to be.

I was nearly hyperventilating by the time I burst into my suite. Slamming the door behind me, I turned the lock and the deadbolt. No visitors, no one to see me falling apart. That's what I wanted. Solitude.

No life remained in the coals inside the hearth. Mist formed in front of me when I breathed.

Frigid. Dark. Good.

It took every last ounce of willpower I had left to trudge across the room and close the window shutters. My elbow knocked into the pot of roses sitting on the sill. Several little petals of sunshine broke away and fell—slowly spiraling down, down, down until they settled onto the cold stone.

An omen.

A sob escaped me as I sat on the edge of my bed. Fingers

shaking as I undid my bootlaces. As I removed my socks, I grit my teeth against the pain as the sodden fabric tore away bits of blistered skin.

Was Emerys in pain, too? Were they torturing him at this moment while I lay here fracturing into pieces? I refused to let my mind linger on the next thought that came to me. I refused to acknowledge that he may not still be alive.

As I pulled back my icy blankets, not bothering to undress, and finally allowed my tears to break free into heavy, ugly sobs. I curled deeper and deeper into the blankets, clutching them to my chest.

I hadn't realized I'd fallen asleep, but I did know I dreamed.

We were on the sea, floorboards of our ship slick as it swayed in the ocean breeze, whipping my hair behind me like a yellow banner. Beside me, Emerys' skin had tanned a lovely gold, making his ice blue eyes that much more stunning. Taking my hand, his lips curled into that sweet, cunning smile I loved so well. I realized then I wanted to kiss him . . . at least once. Just to see what those lips felt like. If they'd make me feel like I hoped they would. I swept his hair away as I leaned in—

—Then my eyes fluttered open as a soft knock rattled my door. The tears began again as it sunk in that I still lay in my bed. Emerys wasn't here, and I may never see him again. Once again, a knock invaded my quiet space. Pulling the blankets over my head, I ignored it.

They came again a short time later, but I didn't answer again, allowing myself to drift away.

A jolt of pain drove me from a deep sleep as someone shook my aching shoulder.

I rolled over to see Catrin sitting beside me, beady eyes softer than I'd ever seen them. Her thin, cracked lips stretched into a smile. "And here I thought you might be dead. How disappointing."

Something in the flatness of her tone chased the sadness

away, just for a moment. "I can't die now. Even as a ghost, I couldn't bear to see you so happy." A heaviness settled over my heart, and I narrowed my eyes. "How'd you get in here?"

Huffing, Catrin flicked a golden key out of her sleeve. "Master key."

"Figures." I sat up against my pillows. "Lord forbid you allow me any peace."

Catrin folded her hands in her lap and let out a sharp sigh. "Peace is sparing in your position." I wanted to coil away as the sadness found its way into her eyes as she said, "Besides, I figured you'd want to hear the news."

Please, no. No more. I swallowed, tongue thick and dry. "Tell me."

Her milky gaze passed over my face, settling on my swollen eyes, my matted hair still tangled with twigs and leaves. "Maybe now isn't the best time."

I straightened further and growled. "Stop pretending you're not enjoying this, and just tell me."

"You think I enjoy the fact my so—" Catrin paused, and I thought she might slap me. "My prince is gone, and you're a hateful witch if you think that I could find any joy in this."

She almost called him her son. "Of course not," I exhaled. "That's not what I meant. Please, what news?"

Her back hunched as if she couldn't bear the weight of her words any longer. "The King's men were spotted on the main road by the next village over. They'll be here by morning."

Lord, please, no. I crossed my arms over my chest, trying to keep my broken pieces together. I couldn't breathe. Traitor tears escaped the corners of my eyes. Catrin made no move to comfort me—not that I expected it. Instead, she glowered at me like I'd just threatened to poison her food. She sniffed. "That's it?"

I wiped my eyes, returning her glare, but stayed quiet.

Scoffing, she flicked her wrist at me. "You're just going to mope around like a grunting sow?"

I let out a harsh laugh. "What else am I supposed to do? If you have any grand ideas, please, I'm all ears."

"What happened to that spirit?" Catrin shook her head. "Where's the girl who defied her prince at every turn? Who wasn't afraid to spit in the face of tradition?"

Did she just compliment me? I wiped my nose. "And here I thought you hated that girl."

Catrin smiled—actually smiled. "Not hated . . . more resented." She leaned back against the headboard and sighed. "I'm getting old, girl, and I'd never thought I'd see the day when I met my match."

I couldn't stop the rough laugh that escaped my throat. "The day I out-match you will be glorious, indeed." The gleam of polished wood peeking out of her apron pocket caught my attention. "What's that?"

"This?" Catrin slipped out a long-handled knife with a short, curved blade. "It's a carving knife."

My eyes widened. I'd seen her with it before—on the steps outside Emerys' suite. At the wedding feast, getting shavings all over Mama's tablecloth. *That cheeky, meddling, brilliant hag.* I glanced up at her, smiling. "You didn't have anything to do with Caddic's hammer, did you?"

"Me?" Catrin placed her hand over her chest and winked, a strange gesture on her face. "How dare you assume I'd meddle in my prince's affairs."

"You're right." I stretched, yawning. "You would never be clever enough to use gifts to woo over the one man that could turn the villagers to Emerys' side. Would Caddic have helped lead the search teams without all that shiny buttering beforehand?" I paused and cocked my head. "Where'd you get the steel?"

Catrin grinned. "Found the hammer in the carriage's storage department. Figured it was worth a shot."

"Brilliant."

With a pained grunt, she scooted closer, taking my hand. "Despite your atrocious attitude—and my best efforts—Emerys cares for you. I can't remember the last time I've seen him smile the way he smiles at you. Don't quit just yet."

I wished she'd go back to insulting me. Her kindness made my battered heart ache all the more. "I let him down," I whispered.

"Not yet, you haven't." Catrin squeezed my fingers.

"They've likely already killed him."

"You don't believe that."

"No." I met Catrin's eyes, and they held me with a burning intensity. I sighed, twisting my blankets. "They'll try to ransom him."

"Then don't make excuses," she said. "You're blunt, rude, and tactless to a fault. Not to mention a giant. How can you use these qualities to change your situation?"

Scanning her face, I swallowed. "I don't—"

I yelped as Catrin slapped my knuckles with the handle of her carving knife, and she repeated, "How can you change your situation?"

I held her gaze, gobbling up the strength of the woman beside me. The power of the woman who'd raised a King's son as her own. Who'd survived decades in the sewage pit known as Aberaron.

But what good have of those parts of me done? In the past, I'd used my loud mouth to frighten people into leaving me alone. When that didn't work, I got in their faces and stood over them until they'd finally backed down. I bullied them, like I did Emerys. *But that was different. I can't scare off an entire army.*

Something clicked. *Not an entire army, no, but what about one man?*

I grinned at Catrin, wild and feral, and threw back my blankets. I nodded toward her knife. "How fast are you with that thing?"

Catrin returned my smile. "Fast as any. Why?"

"I need you to do something for me."

20

"Just another part to play."

Vibrations pulsed in the earth, finding their way through my boots and into my bones. Sucking in a deep breath, I straightened my newly carved crown, numbness spreading through my fingers. *I will not be afraid. I refuse to be afraid.*

It had taken all night, but we'd managed to barricade the main road into Lians with every bit of scrap we could find lying around the village. The villagers quickly joined my cause, thankful for the chance to act instead of waiting around for their impending doom to arrive.

Wynny—God bless her—batted her lashes enough to convince the castle staff to join in. Since the prince's party arrived, there'd been such division. Not since the wedding had our two peoples mingled, but here we were—joined against a common enemy.

Drystan's rallying cries kept their spirits high as our new

defenses grew higher, though his attention never strayed far from Wynny. She didn't fail to return his longing looks.

I wanted them to be happy. I would do what I had to make sure that happened. Together—with Drystan's loving guidance —they drove the wagons in front of the barricade.

Grinning ear to ear, Wynny presented me with my crown, courtesy of Catrin—woven magnolia branches adorned with the likeness of a giant snail. Wynny gently placed the decoration over my hair, and the snail lay just above the center of my forehead.

"Perfect." Wynny giggled behind her hand. "You look so very . . ."

"Royal?" I curtsied even though I'd worn a tunic and trousers. "Elegant?"

"Powerful." Wynny's eyes sparkled. "Beautiful and powerful."

I pulled her into a tight hug, hoping to hide my emotion. "You're my best friend," I whispered. It felt good to say the words. "And if I die, keep Drystan alive."

Again, Wynny giggled. "And you are mine." She pulled back, smiling. "I've never had a best friend, and I'm so grateful to have you now. Don't you worry, I promise to keep his head out of the clouds."

I cocked my head and grinned. "If his is in the clouds, where's yours?"

"Here with you," she whispered. "Show them what happens when you mess with Rhiannon Caddell."

And now I stood my vigil from on top of a wagon, limbs trembling from lack of sleep. A cool mist hung in the early morning sky, sticking my loose waves to my face and neck. As the vibrations grew stronger, I widened my stance, planting my hands on my hips—the picture of confidence.

The trembling spread through my body as dozens of plumed helms crested the hill about a mile down the road. My family stood behind me, arms linked, watching the army approach with solemn expressions.

Drystan stepped forward, close enough that I could hear him whisper, "You don't have to do this."

I refused to look at him, worried he'd see the doubt hidden there. "I do."

He shook his head. "Rhia—"

"Today, my name is Princess Rhiannon, wife of Prince Emerys Beyron," I said slowly, letting the words harden my resolve. "And today . . . today you will address me as such."

Drystan dipped his chin with a slight smile and returned to Wynny's side.

Swallowing, throat dry, I glanced to my left—to the castle sitting high atop the hill in the distance.

My castle. My hill. I hoped Catrin could see me.

The rumble of the oncoming horses turned into full-blown thunder as their hooves struck the compact dirt road. Nineteen, twenty, twenty-one, twenty-two . . . twenty-five men rode toward us in a canter.

I'd hoped the barricade would at least give them pause—I wasn't stupid enough to think it would stop them. That all seemed so ridiculous now that I saw the swords at the soldier's hips, their plated armor.

Why did the King feel the need to send knights to clear out a group of peasants? It's not like we could fight back. *Appearances mean everything to him.* Emerys had said that, and he was right. This was an act meant to intimidate us.

Just like the act I needed to play now.

Once they'd grown close enough that I could make out the men's features, I plastered on that same bored yet cheerful smile I'd seen Emerys wear. I kept myself squared, facing them directly.

The leading rider raised his mailed fist, and the soldiers

behind him slowed. Even without that gesture, I guessed him to be in charge by the extra-large violet feathers on his helmet.

I need—have—*to make the first move.* As the horses came to a halt before the barricade, I let my smile widen and called, drawling, "Well met."

The lead rider's thick brows rose.

I continued, letting a hint of irritation touch my tone. "About time you arrived. We've been expecting you for days." *Please, Lord, let this work.*

The soldiers exchanged confused glances, moisture beading on their steel armor. Before they could get a word in, I inclined my chin toward the leader, picking my nails. "And you are?"

The leader straightened in his saddle, scowling. If he'd been a dog, his hackles would have risen. "Sir Cadogen . . . ma'am. Newly anointed captain of the King's house guard."

My brows rose. "Sir Cadogen?" *It can't be.* "Are you a butcher?"

He blinked with heavy lids. "I—I was. As I said, I'm a captain now. Who are you? Why hasn't the prince greeted us?"

No wonder Wynny didn't want to marry him. It took everything I had not to look back and see if she'd recognized him. Thankfully, something else caught my attention. *House guard—not an actual army.* An army, under law, could be judged by the people. Did that same concept count toward the King's personal security?

Nerves crept into my gut, and I fought to keep them at bay. *What would Catrin do?* Slowly, counting two beats between each step, I moved to the edge of the wagon. Head held high, making him wait as I climbed down and parked myself directly in front of his horse and smiled. "I am Princess Rhiannon, your prince's bride."

More exchanged glances. *I've got them unsettled.* "The Wildmen plaguing these lands attacked Lians, abducting your prince. Not two days past." My smile widened. "You're going to help me retrieve him."

A noise, like an older woman's humming, passed through the men, and it took me a moment to realize what it was—laughter.

Sir Cadogen bit down on his lip to hold back his own. The man beside him—thin and ginger-haired—burst into a full-on howl. "You're Emerys' wife? Look at the size of you! No wonder he was so quick to hop his pony so far south."

"Ignore him," Sir Cadogen said, giving the second man a warning look. "He sometimes forgets his place."

"Does he?" I imagined Catrin, imagined that piercing stare that turned bowels to water. I mirrored it—at the captain, at the man beside him, and watched the doubt flicker in their features. "Either way, you *will* turn your attentions to locating the prince."

"That's just like Emerys, isn't it?" The second man said. "Probably too busy watching the geese to notice a group of savages with a net standing in front of him."

Another wave of laughter. Sir Cadogen didn't seem so sure. I stepped away from the captain, moving toward the second man on his lovely mount—a stocky, large-sized white pony with an enormously bushy mane. I let my lips curl into a cruel smile. "Your name?"

The soldier shared an amused look with his companions, then looked back, his eyes raking over me in a way that made my skin crawl. "Andras."

"Andras," I purred, tasting the syllables. "Step down, please."

Andras' eyes glinted to Sir Cadogen, who nodded his approval. Irritably and with an exaggerated sigh, Andras dismounted. I stepped toward him, still smiling. "Remove your helm."

Another rumble of laughter, which Andras shared, but he did obey. I could almost feel my family's bated breaths.

Andras shrugged his shoulders, sneering. "Princess, if you want a kis—"

I planted my fist firmly into his nose, relishing in the crunch I felt beneath my knuckles.

Screaming, Andras doubled over, cupping his face as blood spewed between his fingers. I ignored his stream of curses as I wheeled on Sir Cadogen. "You will direct these men to the far east end of the village. That's where Emerys was taken."

Before the captain could respond, Andras interrupted and spat blood from his mouth. "Are you mad? You're not the queen—"

I glared down my untouched, straight nose. "While you're in my region, I am your queen."

"The *King,*" Sir Cadogen said, gripping his reins tight. "Sent us to retrieve his payment or lay out the village. That's our orders."

"And when he finds out you left his son to savages?" I tsked. "How will that look to his subjects? They may find his competitors, in other lands or within, to be a more suitable ruler." Honestly, I didn't know if other parties were vying for the throne, but I took a shot in the dark anyway. With six sons, one of them must be hoping for a quick jump to kinghood.

Sir Cadogen paled, chewing his tongue for a moment, before glancing back to his men. Their eyes were as wide and round as his. By the time his gaze returned to me, I'd made sure that my bored smile greeted him. "To the east side, then?"

Sir Cadogen bowed in his saddle. "Lead the way, Your Highness."

"Excellent." I gestured to the still bleeding Andras. "I'll be needing his armor and horse. I'll have my people escort him to the castle. That nose needs tending."

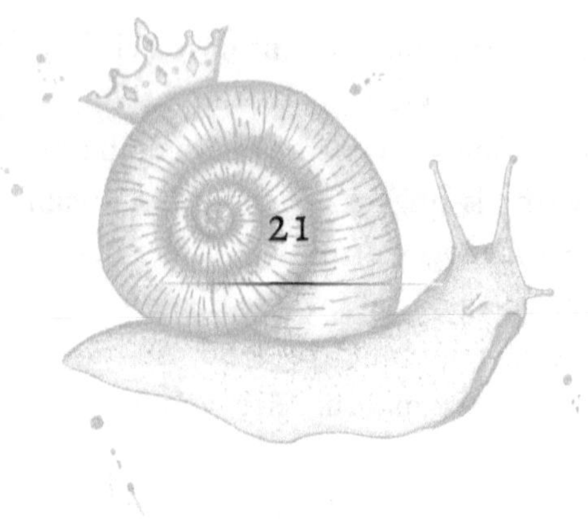

21

"Imposter."

Besides being tight across the chest, Andras's armor fit like a glove.

I wished Emerys could see me now.

Maybe he'd been right about my name. Andras' petite, white mare didn't seem to mind my takeover, and as the group of soldiers followed me across the village on horseback, I caught a glimpse of my reflection in the windows of Town Hall—one of the last buildings with glass. Atop my noble steed, golden braid trailing down the back of my shining silver armor, I could be mistaken for the Great Queen if my legs weren't nearly dragging the ground.

As we headed toward Mama and Papa's hut, the mare jigged beneath me, flipping her head in excitement. I stroked her neck, feeling the coil of her muscles beneath my fingers. *Tiny, yet mighty.* She seemed happy just to be leading the pack, and I envied her confidence.

I wasn't sure how I felt about my new position yet. At this point, I was just thankful no one had driven a knife into my back.

The company stayed surprisingly quiet, except for their eyes, which were sharper than Mama's kitchen knives. Only the sound of the horse's hooves clopping on the damp ground broke the silence. As we reached the edge of my parent's yard, I dismounted to lead the mare on foot.

Sir Cadogen signaled for the soldiers to wait, and he dismounted, following me to the edge of the property. I gestured to the area around us as I chased off a stray chicken. "This is where Emerys was taken. A Wildman chased us from the forest, and we didn't know he had friends with him until it was too late."

Sir Cadogen's dark eyes watched me closely as I crouched, pressing fingers into the prints the men had left behind. "You can see our pursuer's feet are wider and flatter than the others. We followed them until the underbrush had grown too thick for us to continue." I stood, flicking my braid over my shoulder. "That's where we lost the trail."

Sir Cadogen lowered his head, voice soft. "Your Highness, with all respect, we're soldiers, not hunters. Tracking isn't our strong suit."

I was afraid he'd say that. To be honest, part of me hoped the soldiers' presence would be enough to scare the Wildmen into spitting Emerys out of whatever hole they kept him. *Stay calm, Rhia, act the part.* "I don't need you to track them," I said. "I need you to help hack down anyone or anything in my way. Whether it be a tree, bush, or man."

Sir Cadogen jerked his chin toward the sword strapped to the white mare's saddle. "Do you know how to use that?"

Bluff, bluff, bluff. Cocking my head, I smiled. "Do you want to find out?"

To my pleasant surprise, he chuckled. "No, I don't think I

do." Sir Cadogen lowered his head respectfully, and the entire company behind him did the same. "Shall we carry on?"

Throat tight, I mounted the white mare, clunky with the weight of my new armor. *We have to move fast.* Every moment wasted meant a moment closer to the Wildmen cutting their losses with Emerys and disposing of him. Besides that, it was only so long before my new companions realized I'm a fraud—and when they did, they'd probably be furious enough to do what they came to do—destroy Lians.

Squeezing my calves into her sides, the white mare sprang into action. Doing her trademark dance as we passed through the tree line, her steps so graceful that the underbrush seemed to part for her passing.

I turned to Sir Cadogen. "What's this beauty's name?"

The knight's lips twitched in response. "Epona, your highness, named for the Great Queen's equine likeness and bred from the King's finest Welsh ponies." More twitching. "Seems fitting you should ride her now. She never took well to her former master, despite the enormous sum he paid for her. Their personalities were too . . . clashing."

"I wonder why?" I rolled my eyes, then paused. "Former master?"

It was nice to see him smile. "Did you intend to give her back?"

I let out a low, husky laugh then turned back to the forest. Now that he mentioned it, I didn't think I did. Stroking the mare's neck, I whispered. "Epona, is it?"

Epona flicked her ears back in response, and I smiled. *Definitely mine now. Take that, Drystan.*

It was difficult to ignore the feeling of *wrongness* leading a host of King's men into Gwent's sacred forests. Even though Gwent was one of the earliest settled territories, the Wentwood remained mostly unexplored. It ran too deep, too dense to be conquered, yet here I was—leading armed men inside to cut it down.

All for Emerys.

For Emerys.

The company followed me in a single file line, the horses' steps falling into a steady, firm rhythm—one that the Wildmen would hear from a mile off.

I sensed the trees closing in on us, listening, daring me to harm one leaf on their crowns. It made my skin crawl. "Stay alert," I whispered, hoping the trees weren't listening. "Wildmen have been known to attack from the branches, as well as from ground cover."

A couple of the soldiers glanced up at the thick canopy above, throats bobbing.

"You said this space was searched," Sir Cadogen asked, eyes shifting through the tree line. "What do you hope to find that was not found before?"

I honestly had no idea. Throat dry, I swallowed. "When we first searched, the entire village was still in a panic over the attack and kidnap," I replied, keeping my tone even. "I've slept since then. My eyes are fresh."

He nodded, returning to his vigilant watch as if that was an acceptable answer.

I kept my eyes trained on the ground, the sway of Epona's steps calming me. Before the Wildmen started becoming more aggressive in the last years—and he was a few pounds lighter— Papa and I were always in the forest. He'd point out game trails, the animal's movements to and from the water.

There are always signs of life, He'd say. *If you know where to look.*

But where do I look now, Papa? I wished he was here or Drystan. I'd even take Wynny hunting in the woods as long as I wasn't alone. My mind flashed back to the creek when the Wildman emerged from the trees. To the strange shoes he wore, to the flat tracks outside my parent's hut.

He wore strips of hide wrapped around his boots . . . and I bet my life they used them to keep from making tracks in the muck.

So, if not prints, what would they leave behind?

Without stopping, I swung my leg over the saddle and slid off Epona's back. In unison, the company came to a halt. "Your Highness?" Sir Cadogen dismounted, armor clinking as he moved to my side.

I raised my hand, signaling him to wait. Epona either didn't get the message or ignored it because she followed. Plucking at a few stray blades of grass as I surveyed the area. *Lord, don't fail me now.*

There—ask, and you shall receive—a flat, wide impression in the foliage, almost like a large rock had been rolled away. A thrill of adrenaline ran through my blood. "Here." I pointed out the print, trying to keep my excitement contained.

Approaching cautiously, Sir Cadogen peered over my shoulder and frowned. "I don't see anything."

"Here," I repeated, tracing the foot pattern. "At the river, the Wildman wore animal skins over the bottoms of his boots. We can follow these impressions."

The captain gave me an assessing look. "You didn't see these before?"

I nodded, anxious.

"And the brush kept you from searching deeper into the forest?"

Again, I nodded.

Sir Cadogen glanced back to his men, who awaited his orders with baited breaths.

There it was—the doubt. My stomach lurched. *He probably thinks I'm stalling, giving Lians more time to prepare for a fight.* I couldn't give his thoughts the chance to get that far.

I straightened and brushed past him, remounting Epona willed a steeled expression. "If you're too afraid of a few flea-ridden, mangy rotters to continue, then I don't need you. I'll rescue the prince on my own. Wait until the King hears that." I nudged Epona onwards, and her short legs moved into a brisk, determined pace.

My heart pounded as I listened for them to either leave or follow. I wouldn't look back, couldn't look back—not without showing weakness. I closed my eyes, murmuring desperate prayers, and nearly cried out in relief when the rhythm of the horses' hooves resumed their steady beat. My nerves couldn't take much more of this. A few weeks ago, I sat by the fire in my hut, waiting for my future husband's arrival while planning ways to kill him in his sleep and make it look like an accident.

Now I led the King's house guard through the uncharted forest to rescue said husband from the conniving hands of my people's ancient enemy. Thinking of it that way made it seem so heroic.

Life has a funny way of turning things around, doesn't it?

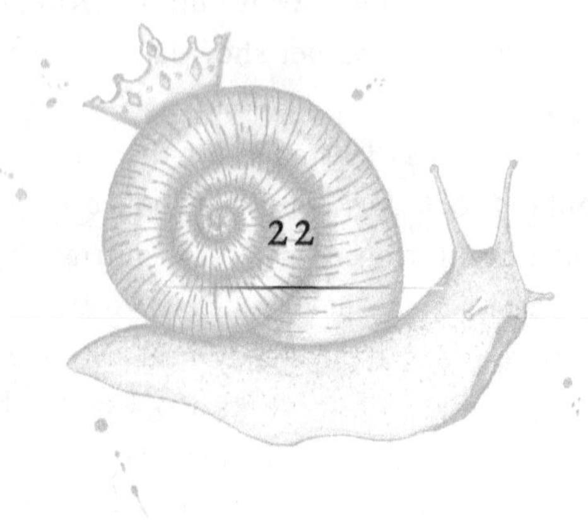

22

"Plans undercover."

The movement of the sun over the treetops told me we'd been out here for far too long—and I didn't know how much longer this game would last.

Trudging behind me, the soldiers began to whisper and grumble, shifting uncomfortably under the weight of their armor. The horses' heads had drooped, the humid air trapped beneath the canopy coating their shoulders in white, foamy sweat.

We have to keep going. After the progress we'd made, I couldn't let them stop. One set of tracks had turned into six, then turned into dozens. Without sharp blades for cutting, my people could never make it this far into the forest. Even with the harshness of the terrain, I felt this was familiar ground for the Wildmen. From my vantage point on horseback, I could barely make out the trails they'd carved for themselves. To them, trekking here was probably as easy as breathing.

The brush and thorned berry bushes were so thick, the soldiers took turns leading the pack, cutting away paths for the horses to walk. Despite Sir Cadogen's loud protests, I'd done my share of the work—and every exposed bit of skin on my body bled for it.

Every muscle ached, and I could barely keep myself straight in the saddle. Only fear kept me going. Fear for Emerys, and fear of when the men behind me decided they no longer wanted to follow.

Epona stumbled, briar catching our legs, and her sides heaved as she slowly regained her balance. I sighed, leaning back to stroke her hindquarters. About an hour ago, her signature jig had slowed to a walk. She needed a break. We all did.

I slid off Epona's back, signaling for the others to halt, and swore she let out a sigh of relief. "We'll rest here."

Another collective sigh. Dismounting, many of the soldiers led their horses to the stream running nearby. I tied Epona's reins so she wouldn't step on them and let her wander off as I sat on a stump. I sipped at my canteen, thankful for a chance to rest my chaffed backside.

Fifteen minutes later, Sir Cadogen removed his helmet as he approached me, sweat dripping down his dirt-stained skin, dark hair matted to his scalp. With a groan, he slumped down on the ground beside me, pouring some of his water over his head. Scrubbing his face, he said. "We've been at this all day. The men are tired. The horses are tired."

I nodded, swallowing. "I know. That's why I'm going the rest of the way on foot."

"Alone?" He seemed surprised.

I smiled. "Are you volunteering to join me?"

Sir Cadogen chewed his lip, deep in thought, then shifted and called a few names over his shoulder. The men to whom they belonged perked up, glancing between themselves before striding towards us.

"We will accompany you." Sir Cadogen huffed. "The rest will guard the horses."

I gave him an approving nod and stood. "Shall we?"

"You don't want to rest longer?" One of the soldiers asked, expression sinking in disappointment, probably wanting nothing more than to head back and kick his feet up while sipping an ale.

"Every second we wait is time they can use to harm the prince." My feet throbbed, and it took everything I had not to hobble as I made my way to the stream. If not for the horde of men, I would have stripped naked and dove into the icy water, even if it was only shin-deep. As I refilled my canteen, Epona trotted to me from across the far bank, water dripping from her muzzle. I cringed as she shoved her slobbery nose into the crook of my neck. *She knows I'm leaving.*

Letting out a long breath, I ran my fingers through her tangled mane. "Stay here, sweet girl. Rest."

She raised her head with a snort, giving me a look I understood all too well—one Drystan had given me a thousand times. *Where you go, I go, too.*

"Fair enough." I kissed the bridge of her nose, looping her reins around my elbow. Without a word, I picked up the trail and headed off again, Sir Cadogen and his chosen soldiers close behind. None of them argued Epona joining our party. In fact, their horses perked up and followed after her. So much for on foot.

After another hour, my sword had completely forgone its identity as a weapon of war and accepted its new humble role as a working man's machete. I grit my teeth, fuming with every swing, bramble flying. *He better be worth it.* Whack. *I swear if he snores, I'm going to give him back to the King.* Crash.

And if he doesn't rub my new bunions every night, he can sleep with the sheep.

The others ducked and dodged my flailing fury, stealth long forgotten.

The forest had grown so dense, I couldn't see a foot ahead, so instead, I kept my eyes on the ground. Focused on the perfect footprints leading the way through the labyrinth of trees. So perfect, one might think this was a—

I froze, glancing back to see Sir Cadogen's wide, nervous eyes. Breathing heavily, I mouthed. *"Don't move."*

The men shifted anxiously. Whickering, Epona nudged at my back. "Stop." I waved her off, and she nipped at my hand. With such firm ground, the prints shouldn't be this deep. Slowly, oh so slowly, I crouched. Running my fingers inside the track, I could feel a hint of moisture where the rest of the ground remained bone dry. I blew out a breath. "Lord above."

"Your Highness?" Sir Cadogen asked.

Straightening, I said. "They wet the ground to make these prints." I surveyed the trees, my heart beginning to race. "They're playing with us."

One of the soldiers groaned. "You mean we've been going all this way for *nothing?*" The others murmured their agreement, tempers rising alarmingly fast. *Oh no.* Here it comes—the imminent implosion of my poorly planned ruse.

Sweat dripped down my temple, my wooden crown digging into my scalp. *Think fast, Rhia.* "Not for nothing," I spat. *I sound like Papa.* "If they lead us this way, it's because they're trying to keep us away from something *else.*"

Sir Cadogen nodded. "You're not wrong."

Trying to hide my relief, I turned back to the tracks as he continued. As I searched the ground, my finger caught on what looked like twine.

"But be careful, Your Highness, there may be tra—"

Yelping, I barely ducked in time to avoid the thick branch

flying toward my head. The soldier nearest to me wasn't so lucky. He screamed—like a pig's *weeting*—as the branch collided into his stomach, scraping against his armor, and sent him flying. His horse reared, tipping over backward into the berry bushes, shrieking. Before I could catch my breath, branches soared in every direction. Crashing into the horses' sides, sending the men airborne, resembling the circus performers that had come to town once.

A loud snap made me look up—only to see a giant rock falling toward my head. *How did they get that up there?* Something hard collided with my side, sending a jolt of pain through my still aching shoulder. My head hit the ground, followed by the crunch of bone, and Sir Cadogen's loud curses split my ears.

My vision swam as I pulled myself up. The rock had Sir Cadogen pinned by the elbow, unable to move as he lay on his back, groaning.

Oh my. I'm ashamed to admit that for a moment, I just blinked at him, completely stunned. *He saved my life.* Breathes shallow, I scrambled over to him, unnerved by how pale he'd become. "What's the damage?" I laid my hands on the stone, and he let out another groan. "Can I move this?"

I expected him to say no, but instead, Sir Cadogen sucked in a few gasping breaths, then growled. "Do it. Get it over with."

Around me, the remaining soldiers pulled themselves slowly from the dirt, attentions immediately on their wounded mounts. A thought struck me in the gut, and my eyes widened. *Where's Epona?* On instinct, I whistled. Once. Twice. Out of the brush, Epona trotted to my side, her legs and stifles bleeding.

Thank goodness. In a moment, I'd worry about her. First, Sir Cadogen needed me.

Either sensing his pain—or just being a troll—Epona snorted in the captain's face, splattering it with freckles of mud. "Stupid animal—" Sir Cadogen's eyes locked onto mine, and he seethed. "Get. It. Off."

"Stop being rude, and I might." I pressed against the stone, voice light, slowly increasing the pressure against it as I pushed. "Don't think this gets you off guard duty."

"I wouldn't dream of it." He grit his teeth, pinching the bridge of his nose with his free hand as I continued to struggle.

I sagged against the stone, breath ragged and cursed. "It's too heavy. I'll get help. Hold on—" A branch snapped—an untriggered trap—and Epona spun frantically as a tree limb slammed into her flank. As she did, her hindquarters collided with the stone, shifting it. Sir Cadogen screamed as the stone slid—*slid,* not rolled—off his arm.

My stomach crawled into my spine as I tried not to vomit at the sound of his bones creaking.

"Bloody beast!" Sir Cadogen leapt to his feet, too fast, then stumbled back to his knees.

Epona whickered happily, pressing her muzzle to my cheek. I patted her, smiling at the captain. "Are you sure this is a pony?"

"She's going to be dog food," He muttered, then surprisingly, burst into pained laughter. "Thank you."

Nodding, I left it at that. *We're even now.*

"Sir!" Panting, one of the soldiers jogged over. "We need to retreat. Too many injuries. We—"

"Head back," I ordered, standing. "Send the others. They'll tend to you at the castle." I turned to Sir Cadogen. "I'll keep going."

He shook his head. "You can't go alone."

"Really? How are you going to stop me?" I nodded toward the rest of the party. "Go with them. You're a mess."

Sighing, Sir Cadogen got to his feet. "Tis' only a flesh wound. I'm coming."

"No, you're heading back."

With his good hand, Sir Cadogen cut a strip of fabric from Epona's saddle blanket, tying on a sling, and smiled. "How are you going to stop me?"

I smiled back and nodded.

As the remaining soldiers limped back into the forest, the captain and I continued onward. It took another hour to push through to the other side of the underbrush. I tried not to think of Sir Cadogen's arm, tried not to think of the blood smeared over my face and hands from the bushes' jagged thorns.

We stepped into a clearing about half a mile wide. The low-hanging sun peeked through the trees, whispering that dusk approached. I breathed in cool air, filled with the scent of wild-flowers, free of the murky humidity under the canopy.

"Well, this is nice." Sir Cadogen slumped against the nearest tree, sweating profusely. I tried to swallow down my guilt. Hopefully, one of Emerys' servants was a skilled enough healer to set his elbow, or he may never have use of it again—because of me.

Epona pulled against the reins, reaching for the meadow's thick, green grass.

Epona. Crouching, I let her eat as I inspected her blood-stained limbs and sides. I ran my fingers through her coat, finding several gashes, but most were shallow and already clot-ting—nothing witch hazel couldn't treat.

"Your Highness?" Sir Cadogen gasped, voice shaking.

I jerked upright, alarmed, and found at least fifty armed men emerging from the forest on the opposite side of the clearing.

They weren't my men.

23

"Fake it until you make it."

Not only men, I realized, but women . . . and very mean-looking dogs.

Every eye—human and animal—pinned us to the spot, daring us to make the first move. *You're so stupid, Rhia.* That nightmare of a trap was merely an appetizer for the main course . . . and I walked right into it—a rabbit in a snare.

A slow clap broke the silence. A man I recognized all too well stepped from the pack, grinning—the Wildman from the creek, the ball crusher. Opening his arms wide, still wearing his deer skins, he burst into a hearty laugh that the group behind him echoed. "I'm surprised you made it this far." He gestured to his right leg, splinted at the ankle. "I still owe you for this."

"I don't owe you cow crap," I hissed, temper flaring in my chest. "You stole my husband. I'd like him back."

Sir Cadogen just watched, focused on every move our aggressor made.

The Wildman shook his head. "You want a man that went and got himself kidnapped?"

I shrugged. "He can be a bit flowery, but he's mine. Where's Emerys?"

Eyes narrowing, the Wildman gave me an assessing look. "I know who you are, but not your name, wench."

I willed my heart to slow. *I need to gain his trust.* "Rhia." I rested my hand on my hip. "And yours?"

"Aron."

"Well, Aron." I flipped my braid over my shoulder. Epona flicked her head, mane flowing in the breeze. "I'd like to speak to whoever's in charge. Seeing that you haven't slaughtered us yet, I assume it isn't you."

"Or maybe I am in charge." Aron smiled, teeth rotten. "And *that's* why you ain't dead yet."

Good point. I arched my brow. Sir Cadogen watched me warily. "Just take me to your leader before I break your other ankle."

Aron laughed, bowing deeply. The pack of Wildmen with him parted. "After you, princess."

Fake it. Just fake it. Head high, hips swaying, I strode through the group, feeling their eyes following me. Their dogs—large-sized mutts—growled and snapped at my knees. A dog lunged for Epona as we passed, yowling as she nailed it with her back hoof, sending it rolling. It limped off, whining, tail between its legs.

I swallowed. *That's exactly how the King's men must have looked getting hit by branches.*

Sir Cadogen caught up to me, holding his elbow as Aron and the pack closed the gap behind us. "I hope you know what you're doing, Your Highness."

"Of course, I do," I whispered back. "I've gotten us this far, haven't I?"

"That you have," Sir Cadogen sighed. "Just . . . be on your guard."

The group of men and women encircled us as we walked, steering us in their makeshift human cage. Another tactic, I realized, to keep us from memorizing the way to their encampment. Too bad for them, I could see straight over their heads.

A well-worn path led out of the clearing, back into the forest. With more stumps and a thinner tree line, the Wildmen must have used this space for logging at some point. Oak trees —just like the ones surrounding Lians. Most of the trees still standing here were birch and ash.

Am I the first of my people to trek far enough into the Wentwood to see this? Is the reason they snuck into my village's border because they'd were running out of good oak for their homes?

As we rounded a bend, the path widened, and a small village opened up in front of us. The shacks sat so densely packed together a person could easily pass a cup to his neighbor through the window.

If you could call them shacks, more like long wood slabs nailed together into a basic square shape. *At least I know what became of our steel.* It had been bent and molded to create patches for the parts of their thatch roofs that were rotting.

Barefooted children and scrawny chickens darted between the legs of the adults leading us. Outside the nearest hut, a tall, reedy man split logs on a chopping block. As we approached, he turned, wiping his brow as he rested his ax against his knee.

The group dispersed, merging into the scenery but still close enough to listen. Aron remained, gesturing to me then to the man with the ax. "You wanted to meet the man in charge? Here he is."

I kept my chin high, my shoulders back. This new Wildman —unlike Aron—had a kind face, if not a bit sickly. His long, greying curls tied back with string, clothes even shabbier than what his comrades wore with holes worn the knees of his animal skin trousers. "Princess." He bowed, smiling, and I realized then I knew him.

"You took Emerys' cloak," I said, stunned. "When we were digging the flats."

"I did." The man grinned. "And as promised, got many pleasurable nights from it, thanks to your prince." When I didn't return his smile, he cleared his throat. "Let me introduce myself —I'm called Harri Moon-Wiggle."

I couldn't help the snorting laugh that escaped me. "Moon-Wiggle?"

Harri's eyes sparkled. "Legend says my mother screamed so loud at my birth that it made the moon wiggle." He spun in place. "Alas, here I am."

"Here you are," I smirked. "But I don't care about you. Where's Emerys? I don't have much patience left after you tried to murder my men and me with those traps."

Harri's brows arched. "Your men?"

A flush crept up my neck. "At the time being."

"I don't see them with you. Just one old, injured knight."

"I've got far fewer years than you, savage." Sir Cadogen growled, still gripping his elbow. "I have armed men waiting on my order. We've come on the order of King Beyron."

Harri leaned to the side, scanning the forest. "I don't see these armed men." Sir Cadogen frowned, making Harri smile. "Tell me, would they run fast enough to save you if I ordered to cut your throats?"

"We're not here to fight." I cut in, palms sweating. "I just want the prince."

"Aye." Harri's sun-lined face tightened. "You know, we set those traps to keep your people out, and yet here *you* are." He clicked his tongue. "To that, you have my admiration, but how can I trust that these 'armed men' haven't come to kill us all, hmm?"

"Because—after all this time—don't you think we'd have done it already?" I asked. "We want to live in peace, same as you." I sucked in a deep breath, steeling myself. "I want my husband. Give him to me, and we're gone."

From the sidelines, expressions fierce, the Wildmen watching inched closer, ready to defend their leader. Sir Cadogen braced, reaching for his sword with his good hand. As a man of honor, he'd cut them down if I asked. I knew it in my heart. Even if it meant he'd die.

The breeze brushed Harri's curls over his bony cheeks as he cocked his head. "But I've grown so attached to him. He's a talker, you know? His funny words amuse me."

I snarled, enunciating each word dangerously slow. "Where is he?"

Harri grinned, gesturing to the semblance of huts behind him. "Follow me, princess."

Without hesitation, I strode toward him, arms crossed tightly over my chest. As Sir Cadogen made to follow, Harri raised his hand, glancing at me. "Not him. Only you."

"Really?" As I straightened, I realized that I stood a good two inches taller than Harri. "You're insane if you think I'm going to let you lead me into a dark alley alone like some air-headed ninny. The captain comes, too."

Harri frowned. "No."

"Yes."

"Why?"

"Because I said so."

Harri let out a hooting laugh, eyes crinkling at the corners. "I like you. I understand now why your prince speaks so highly of you."

I held back a smile as butterflies flipped in my stomach. *Stupid, stupid, focus.*

"Fine." Harri shook his head. "He comes, too." He turned and headed toward the heart of the village. Even with the coming of dusk, it was still a sauna beneath my armor. Sweat soaked my clothes, making them chafe and bunch. It's so petty that all I could think about was how the skin between my thighs burned like a spider bite.

Harri swayed when we walked, not a limp but some old injury. Hopefully, that meant I could put him in the dirt if it came to a fight.

Speaking of dirt—grimy, peckish faces watched us warily as we passed. From their windows, their bare doors—God bless, even from the holes in their rooves. A middle-aged man worked on the outer wall of the nearest hut, hammering on a hunk of sheet metal—the one that was stolen from Mama and Papa . . . and he nailed it will Caddic's missing hammer.

It wasn't anger that built in my chest, as I would have expected, but sadness—a deep, deep generational sadness that I couldn't shake. If it hadn't been for the ongoing leadership of arrogant men, could this poverty have been avoided?

"Ugly, isn't it?"

I looked up to find Harri studying me. He sighed. "I'm sorry for what Aron did. I wasn't aware of his recent raid until after it happened. I assure you he's been . . . disciplined."

A pinch of my former anger flickered. "He and his *friends* destroyed everything."

"And I apologize."

"You think a sorry changes things?"

Sir Cadogen grunted his agreement.

"Can't it?" Harri gestured to a shack, larger than the others, a short distance away. Not grander, by any means, but a meeting place. He continued. "Where do we start but with an apology?"

The building didn't even have a door. Harri pulled aside strips of heavy leather so we could enter. My lips pursed. Winter would be here before long . . . in these conditions, they wouldn't survive another cold season. Not at this rate.

A beautiful, bright booming laugh struck me as I passed

through the doorway. That laugh could set my blood on fire, bring tears to my eyes. I knew then the answer to the question he'd asked, the one I'd been too scared to answer.

Sitting at a round table with ten other men and women, his back was to me. They howled in laughter, heads thrown back in response to whatever joke or story he'd just told, slamming their mugs against the table. Instead of ale, the liquid that spilled from their cups was only water.

I took in the gleam of his black-brown hair in the low light. His slim build—so at odds with the survival-hardened bodies of the people around him. These must be Harri's warriors.

Emerys wheeled at the sound of the leather flaps and blinked as his ice-blue eyes met mine, lighting up brighter than any star. He stood, rushing forward as if he meant to embrace me, but froze when he noticed Sir Cadogen at my side.

The captain bowed. "Prince, I'm relieved to find you in good health."

"And you, Cadogen." Emerys smiled weakly "Why are you here? Lians—"

"We came for the village, yes." Sir Cadogen paused, briefly glancing between Emerys and me, then smiled. "But to be honest, Your Majesty, your wife terrifies me."

Emerys' lips curled into a sheepish smile. "I understand. She frightens me, too."

Another pause, followed by Harri's soft chuckles, then the entire room followed suit, howling again. From the heat in my cheeks, I knew I was blushing. I crossed my arms, holding my head high. "I trekked all this way, somehow convinced these brutes not to kill me—" I jerked my thumb at Sir Cadogen. "—and I find you, what, playing cards?"

One of the women at the table—even bigger than me, dark hair in dreadlocks—raised her cup. "Care to join, princess?"

Emerys finally took those final steps, taking my hand and gently pressing his lips to the wounds on my palm. My throat grew so tight, I couldn't breathe. I grabbed his torn shirt, pulling him tight against me, despite my armor. Emerys wrapped his arms around me, pressing his face into my shoulder, letting out a hoarse laugh. "You look ravishing in that, by the way."

"I'm sorry." I inhaled the sweet, clean scent of his hair, his skin. "For everything."

"So am I." Emerys pulled away, studying my face. "We've both made mistakes, and no one more than me." He turned, gesturing to Harri, still standing in the doorway, smiling. "This man and I have been doing a lot of talking, and I think we've reached an understanding."

"Understanding?" I asked. "Of what? Raiding and thievery?" But as I said the words, my anger lost heart. Not with the faces of the starving children outside planted in my mind. I turned to Harri, and he tensed. I exhaled. "Yes, we have reached an understanding, haven't we? And as much as I'd like to cave your face in—no offense—I couldn't. Not with what I've seen today."

"We've all done evil things to each other," Harri replied, eyeing Sir Cadogen specifically. "That's life. We all have to survive, one way or the other, and survival is ugly."

"Survival *is* ugly," I repeated, feeling a weight lift from my shoulders. Every one of us was the child of circumstance, but that didn't mean it trapped us. Doomed to play the cards given to us forever.

No—we could change . . . I could change.

"Agreed." Emerys watched me, hesitant, then said slowly. "Which is why I've offered Harri's people sanctuary."

Shock—pure shock rocked my core, but not in a terrible way. It must have shown on my face because Emerys blurted. "In return for helping to repair the damage they've done. They will not survive. You saw it." He nodded to Sir Cadogen. "As did you. The people of Lians aren't faring much better, but with enough manpower and determination? We can do better than survive . . . we can thrive."

"The King expects his dues," Sir Cadogen said, sorrowful, more to me than anyone. "I can't stop your father. I can't disobey his orders."

"He's not asking you to," I said, heart breaking, but I understood. "Destroy Lians. Burn it to the ground if you have to, but we will rebuild. The King can't stop us from doing that, not without killing us."

Sir Cadogen's face dropped. He turned to Emerys, who gave him a confirming nod, then said. "You've always been better than your father. I'm glad someone finally sees it." He turned to me, taking my hand. "And if this is to be my duty, Your Highness, I will not enjoy it."

"Well." A tear escaped down my cheek, and I wiped it away. "Who says we can't celebrate before the destruction begins, hmm?" I faced Harri. "Will you join us, as well? Ask your people. Bring anyone that wants to come. We don't have much, but we'll share what we have."

Harri winced, sucking in a breath. "I don't think your father will like that very much. Or your brother. Or your muscly blacksmith friend. I don't feel like having my skull bashed in."

I rolled my eyes. "They're not in charge anymore. Besides, the only one allowed to bash skulls is me."

Harri glanced to his warriors at the table, whose faces all brightened into beaming, hopeful smiles. What a miracle Emerys had done on them.

Letting out nervous laughter, Harri scratched his balding head. "A party it is, then?"

As the group burst into cheers, Emerys laced his fingers through mine, and I gripped them tight. He smiled at me with such warmth that my insides began to smolder.

I wouldn't lose him again.

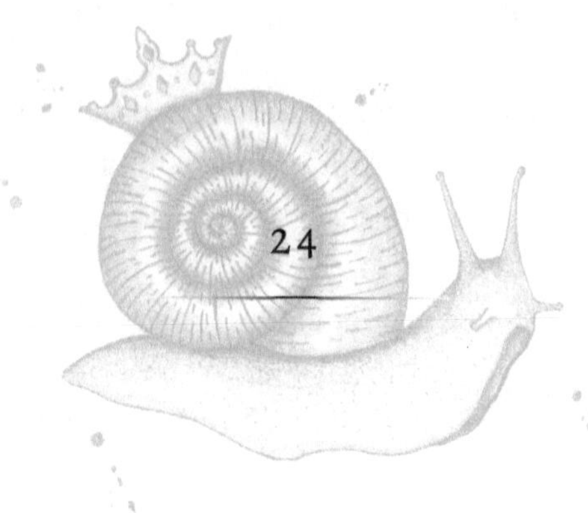

24

"Men are simple creatures."

"**I** knew it." Drystan shook his head, backing away as we emerged from the forest, gripping a makeshift club. "I'd accepted the fact that Mr. Princey-Pants was a lunatic—" He glared at Emerys, who scowled in response. "—but you, Rhia? What have you done?"

An entire village's worth of people stood behind me. Had *followed* me—followed Emerys—because we'd promised them a chance of making it through the coming winter. I didn't have time for Drystan's crap attitude.

Harri peeked over my shoulder, twiddling his fingers at my brother. "Hello, pretty boy. Couldn't catch me the last time we met, could you?"

Drystan bristled like a growling sheepdog. "What is he *doing* here, Rhia?"

"Shut your yap holes, both of you," I snapped. My entire body ached. "I don't want to hear it."

"Where's Mayor Caddell?" Emerys stepped forward, wearing his royal mask.

"Gathering the others," Drystan said. "We were about to send out a search party . . . and now I find you crawling out the dirt with the enemy."

"From where I stand," Harri chirped in. "You look like the enemy, boy."

Drystan lunged for the Wildman, but when I raised my hand, he froze mid-stride. "Get Papa," I said more softly. "There's a lot to talk about, and here isn't the place for it."

When Drystan's eyes met mine, it took everything I had not to crumble at the betrayal I saw there. Stiff as a board, he bowed at the waist. "Anything for you, *princess*." Once he'd turned on his heels, storming off back toward Lians, I finally took a breath.

Creeping up on my right, Harri chuckled. "We're all gonna die."

"Thank you for your un-ending confidence," I replied. My knees buckled as exhaustion settled on my bones. Emerys caught me by the elbow before I hit the ground. Behind me, Epona let out a concerned nicker. Emerys wrapped his steady arm around my waist, pulling me close. "Do you want to ride the rest of the way?"

I shook my head. "She's endured enough of my backside." I gestured to one of the soldiers with Sir Cadogen. "Take her to the pens with the other horses, would you? Make sure she's fed and watered."

"Your Highness." The soldier bowed, taking Epona's reins, but she resisted. Smiling, I stoked the bridge of her nose, over her eyes, and she pressed her muzzle into my neck. "Please, don't kill your new friends, and remember," I whispered to her. "You're mine now."

The little white pony gave me a look that seemed to say. *"Silly human, I chose you."* With that, she allowed the soldier to lead her away, swishing her tail like a woman might swish her hips.

Emerys blew out an exasperated laugh. "Are you sure that's a real animal?"

"I'm less and less sure as time goes on," Sir Cadogen grunted, then turned to me. "As I'm also unsure that it was a mere coincidence you were chosen to become princess. Today may be the first in history that our three parties meet under one roof."

"Don't get too excited," I sighed. "We haven't met yet."

"Let's get to the castle," Emerys said. "You need to rest, and I need a bath."

"Please." I rolled my eyes, then sniffed his shoulder. "You're the cleanest dirty person I've ever met."

Emerys gave me that cute sheepish smile. "I'd rather be the cleanest-clean person you know." He glanced to Sir Cadogen. "And the captain here needs his arm tended to."

Sir Cadogen tried to flex his fingers and winced. "I'll be fine. My armor took most of the damage. It's not as bad as it looks."

"I doubt that," I said and rolled my eyes. "Men."

I could barely walk by the time we passed through the portcullis and into the central courtyard. Dozens and dozens of Wildmen, women, and children packed in behind me, filling the small space. Only the presence of Sir Cadogen and his men kept us from being ambushed on the way through the village. That, and I think Drystan hadn't yet informed them of my intentions. As far as the villagers knew, I'd dragged the ancient enemy to my castle on the hill to throw them into the dungeons.

Do I even have a dungeon? Questions for later.

A low husky laugh caught my attention, and I turned. Catrin stood atop the stairwell leading to the keep, thin lips spread into a wide, wrinkled smile as she watched the crowd pour in. "You did it, girl."

I straightened my magnolia crown, the one she'd carved for me, and grinned. "*We* did it."

To my infinite delight, she grinned back.

"Catrin!" Emerys zipped past me, sprinting up the stairs and wrapping his arms around the older woman, lifting her off the ground. "Please, tell me you didn't murder anyone while I was gone."

"Put me down, stupid boy." Catrin whacked him in the head with the butt of her carving knife. "You're making a fool of yourself in front of your trout wife."

"We love you, too, you crotchety old sack," I called, and she shot me a rude gesture.

"Princess?" I turned to find Harri watching me anxiously. "Do you mean to trap us here and slaughter us all?"

I patted his shoulder, giving him a sweet smile. "With what? You stole our weapons."

"Fair enough." He shrugged. "But in all seriousness, what would you have my people do here?"

It took a moment for me to realize this grown man—a leader and warrior—was genuinely asking me—a clueless sixteen-year-old girl—for direction and not being condescending. *What should they do? What should I do?*

"Let them stay here, safe, for the time being." Emerys returned to my side, smiling brightly. "I'll have my servants bring refreshments to keep them sated until we can meet with Mayor Caddell."

Harri nodded, satisfied, and gestured toward the stairwell. "Lead the way, then."

I took Emerys' elbow as we headed for the stairs, Harri and Sir Cadogen following behind and whispered. "Part of me wants to smack you for interrupting . . . but thank you."

"You're welcome . . . I think. You looked like a deer waiting for a hunter to put an arrow in its side. I thought I'd step in." Emerys smirked. "Besides, I like the idea of us working as a team."

I studied his face as we walked down the hall, watching the

way his eyes darted to the windows as a sparrow fluttered past. Kind. Soft. None of the tempered anger worn by so many rulers —and by me.

Balance—he balanced me. I smiled. "We do make a good team, don't we?" When he smiled back, I said. "Which is why you'll be leading this meeting."

Emerys seemed surprised. "Really? How generous of you."

"Don't make me change my mind." I grinned, our footsteps echoing on the stone floor. "These men need to respect *you* for this truce to work. Plus, nothing would make me happier than for your father to find out you ended a centuries-old war that he couldn't touch."

Emerys inhaled. "You did that, not me."

"Did I?" I shot back. "No, you did that when you chose to think instead of act when we were approached on the mudflats. Be that person. Wear your mask."

"My mask?" His brow arched. "What mask would that be?"

"The face of a confident royal diplomat that may also be a trout."

Emerys laughed, sweet and lovely. I reached out and squeezed his hand. "Save the bird-loving, rock collector face for me."

He squeezed my fingers back, smiling. "Only for you."

"Rhia! Emerys!"

As we rounded the corner, headed toward the keep, Wynny came sprinting towards us, slipping on the hall's polished floors. Emerys' cheeks turned bright pink as she crushed us in a tight hug, weeping into our shoulders. "I thought you both were dead! Oh, my goodness, never leave me like that again—" As she raised her head, glancing behind us, and her eyes widened.

Looking back, Emerys wasn't the only one blushing. Sir Cadogen's face went crimson. She stared at him, and he bowed awkwardly. "Er, Lady Beyron."

Wynny curtsied, equally stiff. "Cadogen."

"Moon-Wiggle!" Harri raised his hand. "Harri Moon-Wiggle, my lady, and may I say, you are divine." Wynny burst into giggles, mouth shielded behind her palm. Sir Cadogen gave Harri a scathing look as he continued. "Would you like to ride with me beneath a full moon? It would pale in comparison to your beauty. I will—"

"She's taken, you wrinkled turnip peel." I tucked my arm through Wynny's, flipping my braid over my shoulder.

"Yes." Another giggle escaped as Wynny huffed. "Rhia and I are going to be sisters."

"That's right, I—" I blinked, and Emerys and I spoke in unison.

"*What?*"

Beaming, Wynny waggled the fingers on her left hand. On her third finger lay a smooth, polished wooden ring. "Drystan asked me to marry him, and I said yes!"

Silence.

Emerys and I exchanged glances, a dozen emotions passing between us before I bent over, roaring with laughter. Wynny crossed her arms, scowling, as I gasped in jagged breaths, wiping tears from my eyes. "I should have known when you caught the pin at the wedding!" Wynny relaxed as I took her hands and allowed myself to squeal with her as I asked. "When? Did he ask your father? Of course, he didn't ask your father. Did he ask my father? My mother? Tell me!"

"Rhi-Rhi?" The voice was low but hinted with amusement.

Papa stood in the doorway of the keep, Drystan at his side at the end of the hall. My brother managed a small smile seeing me with his soon-to-be bride, despite the tension filling the room.

Papa's wooden leg clacked against stone as he stepped closer, eyes locked on Harri. "Moon-Wiggle." Papa patted his leg. "I haven't seen you since I lost this."

Harri spread his arms, head cocked. "Sorry, Caddell. That sickle was sharper than I expected."

Papa grunted with a nod. "It was pretty sharp, wasn't it? Almost died from infection, I did."

Harri pulled back the collar of his rabbit-skin shirt, revealing a lumpy scar on his shoulder. "Maimed or not, you have excellent arm when throwing butter knives."

With another grunt, Papa waved us on. "Well, there's no use arguing with my stubborn daughter. Let's get this over with."

Drystan ignored me as Emerys and I stepped into the keep, my palms slick against the prince's, and he gave my hand a reassuring squeeze. Wynny whispered a few words to her fiancé before shuffling off. My eyes followed her down the hall and found that Mama and Catrin were waiting for her. Mama winked at me, wringing her hands. I gave her a nervous smile back.

The tables and chairs had been stacked against the walls, leaving only one table on the dais waiting for us. Our footsteps seemed so obnoxiously loud as we headed across the room, candlelight casting shadows over the stone floor.

Emerys sat at the end of the table, Papa sitting opposite. The rest of us piled in on the sides and waited as the two men stared each other down. Emerys' expression remained calm and bored as Papa steepled his fingers, blond mustache twitching. "Son, I heard you offered these savages sanctuary in my village."

Emerys merely shrugged. "I did."

"Why?"

"Because he can," Harri cut in, winking at me. "He's the prince, isn't he?"

I swallowed, fists clenched on my lap, waiting for Papa to explode.

Papa's nodded slowly, eyes narrowing. "He is. What a change that's been." He glanced at my hands, entwined with Emerys', then to Wynny waiting in the hall. He sighed. "Seems a lot has changed of late."

Harri nodded. "We all gotta keep up with the times, don't we? I'm getting old and tired of fightin'."

I exchanged edged glances with everyone at the table, sweat dripping down my sides.

Papa harrumphed. "Tell me," He shifted his chair, facing Harri. "How are you at brewing ale?"

Harri leaned in, smile deadly. "Let me tell *you,* old man—"

And that was that.

I nodded off in my chair as the men talked long into the night. At some point, I woke and found myself in my own suite, laying on my own mattress under my thick warm blankets. I rolled over and found Emerys fast asleep on the floor beside my bed, dark hair covering his eyes. Smiling to myself, I laid a blanket over him and went back to sleep.

Miracles could happen, after all.

25

"On the subject of mollusks."

Two nights later, as the moon rose in the sky, the south yard lay transformed into a fairy garden so grand the Great Queen herself would be jealous—thanks to Mama and Wynny.

And if it weren't for Catrin's lingering violent stares as she lumbered through the halls, the castle would have fallen into turmoil. In those two days, Drystan had tackled Harri to the ground when he blew a kiss at Wynny. Caddic threatened that if Aron didn't return his tools, he'd bash the Wildman's face into his anvil. After a lot of yelling and posturing from Emerys and me, we'd survived the hours it took to ready the feast—but only just.

Tomorrow, Sir Cadogen and his men would return to the King in Aberaron . . . and wipe Lians off the map as they departed.

But that was tomorrow, and today we would eat and be merry.

Guests packed the courtyard to the brim—probably for the first time in Lians' history.

Full of life, full of laugher . . . and cursing, and fighting, mixed with dancing and bawdy songs. Everything a Welsh fairy night should be. Even the King's soldiers were joking and drinking with the rest.

I stood in the stairwell, adjusting to the chill in the air. While lovely, my new gown was certainly not warm with its wide lace neckline and train, silver flowers, brocaded on the deep green bodice, matched the silver twine Mama added to my crown.

"You are beautiful."

I turned, and Emerys stood on the landing above me, wearing the same black and gold cape and doublet he wore at our wedding. Sneering, I turned back to the party, letting my fingers trail over the railing. "I can't believe you're wearing the same outfit twice."

Chuckling, Emerys moved down the stairs to stand beside me. "Maybe you've taught me some modesty."

"You were always modest."

He snorted. "And you aren't?"

I waggled my brows at him, and he laughed—my favorite sound. Grinning, I reached for him. "Care to dance?"

He smiled back. "You're a romantic?"

"Is that a bad thing?"

"Depends." I squealed as Emerys swooped me up into his arms, carrying me into the center of the yard. The crowd cheered, spilling their ale, as he took my hand, bowing as he pressed a light kiss to my knuckles. "I'd love to dance."

And so we did, for hours—all of us.

We danced until my braids came loose, letting my golden waves spill to my hips. Danced until Mama helped Papa limp to the nearest chair, his face flushed. Danced as Wynny wrapped her arms around Drystan's neck and he whispered to her sweet nothings, their foreheads pressed together.

As we slowed beneath the magnolia tree, Emerys twirled me until he held me snuggly in his arms, pressing his lips gently against my neck. "I'm glad to know you, Rhiannon Caddell."

I faced him, shaking my head violently as the press of his body against mine made my core burn.

Emerys grinned, stroking my chin. "What is it that you don't want to be thinking about?"

So many things, but you only need to know one. I smiled back, brushing my fingers over his cheek, warm from movement, and let my voice fall to a mere breath. "That I love you. And I, too, am glad to know you, Emerys Beyron."

Emerys opened his mouth to answer, eyes glittering, when we were interrupted by Catrin's croaky voice as she called to the guests. "Time to eat, you greedy slugs!"

We were swept into the storm of hungry bodies and plopped at the head of the main table. Servants ducked in and out of the rows of smaller tables, faces flushed, and laid out steaming bowls of stew alongside plates of hot bread and homemade butter. Simple fare, but all we had left, especially for such a large crowd.

Across our table, Papa and Harri roared with laughter, patting each other's backs, heads in their cups. Drystan and Wynny fed one another bites of bread, brushing noses. Catrin and Mama argued over napkins.

This . . . this is what I wanted—forever—but we'd be losing it all when morning came. I shook my head. *Don't think about it now.* Emerys' fingers brushed my side, sensing my sadness.

When they laid out our food, I jolted in horror as a familiar scent hit my nose—snail stew. They were serving snail stew to the *King's* men.

Dear, God, save us. I leapt to my feet, hips knocking into the table, spilling my wine. Shocked, Emerys touched my arm. "Rhia, what's wrong?"

I scanned the crowd, breathing heavily. *Where's Sir Cadogen? I couldn't let him eat it.* I spotted him. *There—two tables down.*

"Rhia?" Emerys followed me as I sprinted toward the captain's table. I tripped on the train of my gown, knees hitting the ground, just as Sir Cadogen spooned soup into his mouth, his bad arm wound tightly in a sling.

"Rhia, what is it?" Emerys pulled me to my feet, expression reflecting the fear in mine. I couldn't move. Shaking, I watched as Sir Cadogen chewed and swallowed, eyes widening as he looked down at the steaming bowl in front of him.

Please, no. I pulled away from Emerys' grip and reached the captain's table. "I'm so sorry. It's a local dish. You weren't supposed—"

"This is extraordinary, Your Highness." Sir Cadogen took my hand. "You must tell me what it's called."

Emerys and I exchanged glances. "I-it's just *cawl*," I stammered. "Made with snails, instead of beef. We don't have any cows to spare."

"I've eaten with more lords and ladies than I can count," Sir Cadogen said. "And I've never had anything this wonderful."

"It *is* wonderful, isn't it?" Catrin appeared at Emerys' elbow, making him jump. "Can you imagine those court ninny's faces if they realized the delights of common fare?" She twirled a spoon between her fingers. "I bet they'd pay their weight in the King's gold, just to get a taste."

"There aren't enough snails in the west to support royal appetites," I laughed. "Only in Lians—"

Catrin gave me a knowing look. My jaw dropped. *That little—*

Caddic's hammer, my crown—she'd known all along.

Emerys must have realized the moment I had because he wheeled on Sir Cadogen, nearly bursting with excitement. "Can you delay your return trip for a week? With all of Lians new citizens, I bet we can gather a *gift* large enough for the King's private court. Maybe, even enough for a first tax payment?"

I'd never seen a wider smile than Sir Cadogen's, as he said. "Aye, I think we can manage that, prince. Anything for the new queen of Lians."

"I'm not a queen," I laughed. "That . . . that was a bad bit of drama on my part."

Sir Cadogen stood from the table, moving so he could kneel at my feet. "In Gwent, in any region, you are my queen."

"And mine." Emerys ran his fingers lovingly through my hair. "Rhiannon the Great Queen."

A soldier banged his cup against the table, and I realized then it was Andras, his nose still swollen from where I punched him. "All hail the Great Queen!"

The cheer rippled through the crowd, and I nearly burst into tears when Catrin joined in. Mama and Wynny danced to the tune around the table where Papa and Harri had passed out drunk, snoring.

Drystan stepped to my side, wrapping an arm around my shoulder, then shrugged. "You'll always just be Rhia, my annoying sister, to me."

"Good." I hugged him. "That's all I wanted from the start."

Once stomachs were filled and the hours continued, cheers returned to bawdy songs as the Wildmen danced on the tables, arm in arm with Emerys' servants. My people sat around the bonfire, trading stories with the soldiers.

I searched for Emerys and found him above in the stairwell, gazing over the yard. I trotted up the stairs and was breathless when I made it to the top. He gave me that cheeky smile as I approached, eyes bright. "I thought of a name for the castle."

"Oh?"

"Narberth." His smile widened into a grin. "Let the story-tellers decipher that one."

I shook my head. "That's morbid."

Emerys just continued to smile, a pink flush coloring his cheeks.

"What?" I smiled back, heat crawling up my neck. "You're staring."

"I can't help it." He lowered his eyes back to the party below. "It looks like we've reached happily ever after."

I sidled up next to him. "Not yet."

He raised a brow. "No?"

Every part of my body caught aflame. "You haven't kissed me, you mad milksop."

Eyes full of laughter, with hope—with everything I never knew I needed—Emerys wove his fingers through my hair and pressed his lips to mine.

Gently at first—until I kissed him back.

Lord above, I love snails.

That's really the sum of it.

NOTE FROM THE AUTHOR

Congratulations! If you made it this far, you have my absolute gratitude! The process of starting a novel and taking it all the way to publication is a whirlwind, and I can't thank you enough for riding it with me!

I'd love to hear all your thoughts and feedback, so feel free to contact me at brittanytuckeryaauthor@gmail.com or reach out on any of my social media platforms.

The greatest way you can help me on my journey is to please leave a review on Amazon and Goodreads! Reviews are necessary to stay in the algorithm and help my stories reach more readers. I would love to keep in touch so you can be first in line for future content and give-aways, so don't forget to sign up fo my mailing list!

You guys mean the world to me, and I couldn't do this without you!

Love,
Brittany

ACKNOWLEDGMENTS

Of course I have to start with my overwhelming gratitude to the Lord. He opened doors that I could NEVER have opened on my own and shoved me through them. It's honestly so humbling.

Thank you, Corey. Thank you never giving up on me, despite all my wild and failed ideas, and being my ride or die to the end.

Thank you to my baby Lily for showing me what real confidence and beauty is.

Mom, Dad . . . there are no words. Thank you for always letting me be me, and never forcing me to be someone else.

Grandaddy, you unknowingly fed my love of stories and culture with just your very presence. You always believed the best in me, and always pushed me to become more than I ever dreamed I could. I love you.

JC Admore, you knew you'd be here. You've been my Yoda for years and taught me more than any textbook ever could. You're sharp for an old fart.

Jensen Reed, Celeste Bokrony, Hannah Deurloo, Carolyn Young, and Kimberly Mullins—this story would never be what it is without you.

ABOUT THE AUTHOR

Brittany Tucker lives on an island off the coast of Washington state with her husband, daughter, a menagerie of fur-children, and her imagination. She prefers generic cereal, collects tattoos and action figures, and was in the top 5% on the planet for ship's sunk in *Assassin's Creed III*.

Brittany also likes to write books from time to time.

facebook.com/BTuckerAuthor
twitter.com/BTuckerAuthor
goodreads.com/btuckerauthor